New Beginnings - Book 2

Prophet X, Volume 2

David Johnson

Published by David Johnson, 2024.

This is a work of fiction. Similarities to real people, places, or events are entirely coincidental.

NEW BEGINNINGS - BOOK 2

First edition. May 2, 2024.

Copyright © 2024 David Johnson.

ISBN: 979-8224414260

Written by David Johnson.

Table of Contents

New Beginnings

A Novel by David Johnson

2$^{\underline{nd}}$ edition (September 15, 2023)

PUBLISHED BY:

DJ's Artificial Brain, Inc.

Copyright © 2010 by David Johnson

Forward

This is the second book of the *"Prophet X"* book series. In this continuation of the "Prophet X" story, John Davidson and his family try to start over after being relocated from Houston, Texas to Gulf Shores, Alabama. As they settle into their new life things begin to return to normal. But then, the brother of an old enemy suddenly appears. Dangerous people and dangerous situations seem to hunt and find John, no matter where his family goes. When one threat is neutralized, another one seems to appear. To protect his family, John is once again faced with making extraordinary, tough, decisions. A new beginning seems to be just another chapter in the deadly life of the Davidsons.

Where possible I have used real places and technology that I am very familiar with. All character names are purely fictional. Any similarities to actual people are purely coincidental and unintentional. The technology depicted and it's use is based on real world capabilities that currently exist.

~~~

In Memory of Dr. Danny McCarthy (Doc)
09/06/1950-09/11/2023
A great boss and friend
~~~

Chapter 1

~

It had been eighteen months earlier when John and Rhonda Davidson left Texas and everyone they knew behind. They had cut all ties with their friends in Texas. They occasionally phoned their family. But they didn't tell anyone where they were living. Their new place in Gulf Shores, Alabama was starting to feel a little more like home every day. It was a typical coastal lifestyle, with beautiful beaches, warm weather, and a relaxed atmosphere. They had quickly gotten to know the area and had even found a small church to attend. As instructed when they were relocated, they stayed away from creating any close friends for a few years. They weren't in the witness protection system. But the CIA had taken steps to make it much more difficult for anyone to find them.

Their three-story beach house had a large wooden deck that looked out over the sand dunes to the Gulf. The house had light colored siding, metal storm shutters, and a metal roof. The ground floor was comprised of the two-car garage, storage room, and utility room. The second floor is where the kitchen, dining room, den, and a small office were located. On the top floor the bedrooms and full baths were located. The master bedroom had a commanding view of the Gulf at the rear of the house. The front yard was a mixture of sand, tall grasses and bushes that were typical for the coastal area.

From his home office, John sat in on CIA operational conferences, via phone, almost every day. He read reports and made recommendations. Whatever happened downstream from his recommendations he seldom knew. Overall, this job was much easier and very different than working at the utility company. He missed the daily interaction with co-workers, but the money was good, and he worked almost exclusively from home. He was still working for the utility company and did get to talk with some of his co-workers every week. But that too was all done remotely. Between the two jobs he was pretty busy. Often working late into the night on various projects.

Rhonda was still able to work from home as a corporate travel agent. At the CIA's strong suggestion, she had moved from one travel firm to another when they had left Texas. She no longer talked to the clients on the phone unless there was a problem. She mostly handled cancelled flights, missed flights, and refunds. She had her own desk in the house. Her desk was in front of a large picture window that looked out on the gulf. Despite the triple pane windows and tightly wrapped and insulated house, she could faintly hear the sea gulls on the beach from time to time.

Over the last few months, John had been using his computer skills to explore cryptography (scrambling messages so only the intended recipient could read them). The math and programming intrigued him, and it kept his programming skills sharp. After a while, he developed his own cryptography program. It utilized multiple cryptography routines and techniques to scramble and un-scramble a file. He had developed something like this for securing the Prophet X program files, a few years ago. But this was much more advanced and robust. He was always tweaking the program, adding new modules and routines that made the encryption stronger without sacrificing speed. Some day he hoped to reach out to Luke Morgan, at the CIA, and see if he could get the government types to try and break his code. To John, this was just fun stuff to exercise his mind and occupy his time.

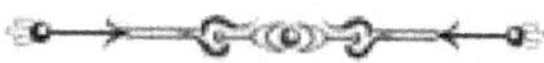

Monday morning John got up early and cooked breakfast. As he sipped his coffee, he cooked a pound of bacon and made some pancakes. A half stick of butter was placed in a Pyrex measuring bowl with two cups of pancake syrup. A minute or two in the microwave melted the butter and heated the syrup. The savory aroma of sizzling bacon was enough to make everyone hungry. During breakfast they talked about their old friends, how they missed them, and wondered how they might be doing. After the breakfast dishes were cleaned and put away it was time for another cup of coffee.

John had just refilled his coffee cup when he received a phone call. A lady named Nancy, in the Houston CIA office, wanted to know if he'd be interested in some training classes in McLean, Virginia. She assured him that the classes, travel expenses and meals would all be paid for in advance. Normally everyone had to wait for a reimbursement check, after submitting an expense report. But the classes would last for a full two weeks, and John was technically just a contractor. John really hated being away from home and two weeks was just too long. John told the lady "Thank you for the offer, but I'm really not interested."

Thirty minutes later John had a call from McGuire, the Director of CIA Operations.

"Hello?"

"John, this is McGuire. Glad I caught you. It's been a while. How's the wife and kids doing?"

"Just fine Mr. McGuire. How are you doing?"

"I've been better. I have a little budget problem and I was hoping you could help me out. I need to spend some major training dollars this month or they'll cut our training budget next quarter."

"So that's what the call this morning was about."

"John, I think this field training class might help you understand the guys here a little better. We all had to go through that class when they hired us, as part of our training. It's normally a four-week class. But this one was put together as a special, abbreviated, training class for people who will interact with but not participate in field operations. Just like you. You'll learn some neat tricks in there."

"I don't know. I've been away from home an awful lot lately. I think I should probably pass on this one."

"John, I was really hoping I could count on you to help me out with this one."

"Well, I'm sure you'll find someone else to go."

"You're right. I could send someone else. But, of all the people in our section, I think you would benefit the most from this training. It's a short course in field ops. This stuff would go right over the heads of most of the other folks I could send. But you catch on quicker than most and you would use the stuff you'd learn in this class more than you think. You'd use it like the air you breath and you wouldn't even realize it. You have no idea how many times I wished we'd found you about 20 years ago. John, you're a natural at this stuff."

"I think you're laying it on a tad bit thick. Don't you? Besides you know how I feel about the methods you guys normally use in field operations."

"John, do you remember that test you took when you started working with us?"

"Yeah. You guys said it was a standard test that everyone had to take. And your point is?"

"Due to your involvement in an active case at the time, there was initially a great deal of opposition to my decision to approach you. The results of the tests you took validated to everyone my decision to bring you on board. In other words, your scores were off the charts in multiple areas."

"So naturally you think I'm too smart to refuse? Let's quit dancing around the tree. What's the real story?"

"John, look, your input has been more helpful to our group than you know. You have talents you do not even realize. I'd just like to see you use them to their fullest potential."

John figured he could afford to burn the two weeks of vacation from the utility company. They were already on the beach. What else could he ask for? Besides, it might be fun.

"McGuire, I know a con job when I hear one. But if it means that much to you..."

"That's great! I'll have Nancy make all the arrangements and give you another call. Thanks a million John. You're a life saver."

John hadn't really intended that to be a 'yes'. But he had been thinking about changing his mind. So, he let it ride.

"Was there anything else?"

"No. I guess that about does it. We'll see you when you get back from Camp Peary and thanks again." And the line went dead.

John knew he had been snookered into doing something he really didn't want to do. Next time, he'd have to hold his ground better when dealing with McGuire. It was only two weeks, and it might be kind of cool to learn some super spy/spook stuff. Besides, he sort of felt obligated to them for pulling him clear of that Prophet X program mess in Texas. Now to tell Rhonda. She wasn't going to like being alone for two weeks.

As they were making the bed John told her about the call from Houston and the trip he had agreed to take. She took it in stride and said she was going to build a new raised flower bed while he was gone. They discussed how and where to get the materials. They decided to use a galvanized water tub from the Farmer Supply store in Foley. It would be placed on brick pavers to keep it out of the sand. Rhonda wanted to paint it red. John told her how to wipe it down with vinegar to get the paint to stick better. She would drill some very small holes in the bottom and put a layer of rock to allow for drainage. The rest was just potting soil and plants from a local nursery.

Three weeks later found John in Virginia, attending classes at Camp Peary. After a day of travel, the plane's wheels finally touched down at Newport News/Williamsburg International Airport. After the plane taxied and came to a stop, the seatbelt sign was turned off and John got his backpack from the overhead compartment. As he exited the plane and stepped onto the jet bridge, the flight attendants thanked him and wished him safe travels. The airport was modern and well-lit with the huge windows that offered views of the planes on the runway and the Virginia landscape beyond.

When he got to baggage claim he noticed a guy holding a sign that said, 'J. Davidson'. After collecting his bag from the baggage carousel, he walked out to the waiting taxis, ignoring the guy with the sign. It was time to have a little fun and spice things up a bit. John had always been a bit of a rebel. As he stepped out of the airport the bright sun was hot and breezy. He had checked the forecast before leaving home. It called for thunder showers to start that night and go into the next day.

Just as John was about to reach for the handle of the nearest taxi, he felt a firm hand grab his shoulder from behind. He turned to see the guy that had been holding the sign. This guy was much bigger up close. John's first impression of him was that he was a body builder. He didn't look amused at all. There was something about this guy that broadcast an unmistakable subliminal message; it said, 'don't mess with me, I will hurt you'.

"Mr. Davidson the sign was so you could identify me. Not the other way around. We have your transportation waiting."

"And if I take a ride with you, where will you be taking me?"

"I am from Camp Peary, and I have been assigned to greet you and help you get sorted out at the base. What do you say we get this show on the road?"

"Sure thing."

So much for John's little fun. This guy was all business and no fun at all.

It was a long, silent, thirty-five-minute ride to the base. At the front gate, they were met by two, armed security officers. John had to sign some papers and was eventually issued a security badge that would get him on to the base. They proceeded to a dorm building and he was shown his room for the next two weeks. It was a modest size room with a bed, desk, closet, and bathroom. It was clean and functional.

After dropping off his luggage, he was given a brief tour of the base; then dropped back at his dorm building. The guy had been kind enough to point out the cafeteria and training buildings. John wasn't looking forward to eating at the base for the next two weeks. The dorm, cafeteria, and training buildings were all within a short walk of each other. Back in his dorm room, John unpacked and went to bed early. Airports and airplanes usually translate into a long day, and he was tired.

The next morning John dressed and headed to the cafeteria for coffee and breakfast. He had opted to skip dinner the night before. As he entered the door, the aroma of breakfast foods was enough to make anyone hungry. It was a large spacious dining area with rows of empty tables and chairs. The cafeteria had only a few diners. He couldn't decide if he was too early or too late for the breakfast crowd. The large buffet had a lot of different foods to choose from and everything looked good. He had two eggs over easy, toast, bacon, and fruit with his coffee.

After a filling breakfast, he made his way to the training building and found the classroom. The classroom looked more like a conference room with its dark panel walls, carpet, and recessed fluorescent lighting. There were six long tables and twenty-eight chairs. The room had dry erase boards, an overhead projector, and a non-descript lectern at the front. It appeared that there were only going to be five students in the class, as there were materials neatly placed in front of five of the chairs, on the front row. The first instructor was a middle-aged black guy. He had a slender build, black rimmed glasses, and wore a dress shirt and jeans. He gave them a brief overview of the class structure and goals. Due to the shortness of the class the materials were to be presented in what the instructor called 'fire hydrant' style. This meant they would be getting a lot of information with little explanation.

Over the next two weeks there was a parade of instructors that came in, one after the other. John and his classmates didn't talk much.

They all seemed to think that the less they knew about each other the better. That was fine by him. But, as the classes progressed, it became apparent that none of his classmates were acquainted with CIA type operations. Indeed, as McGuire had said, the information was familiar to John, but seemed to be totally new concepts for his classmates. The instructors frequently had to stop and explain a concept to one of his classmates. Throughout the classes there would be different instructors brought in to explain various concepts and tactics used in field operations. John supposed these people had a particular expertise in these areas. Much to John's relief, they had been told that, due to time constraints, basic self-defense, hand-to-hand combat, and pistol shooting training would not be covered in these classes.

One section of the classes was devoted to teaching the value of recognizing, creating, and keeping options. It occurred to John that even now he instinctively made decisions and observations that were designed to give him options should he ever find the need to run again. Nothing drastic, just little things, like keeping a small stash of money in his house, having an up to date will, paying cash for most everything, giving out very few personal details to casual friends or the local businesses he dealt with. Living on the Gulf coast had prompted a few preparations in case a hurricane caused an evacuation. These same preparations could also be useful if he had to leave for any other reason as well. He knew all the routes out of their neighborhood. He had made it a point to familiarize himself with all the back roads from their house to about fifty miles inland. Most of all he paid closer attention to details in his surroundings. Little things like knowing the color and make of all the cars that normally lived on their street. He wasn't paranoid, he didn't suspect anyone, he just approached life with more caution than before. He supposed that once a person has had to live looking over their shoulder, that they continue to do so, to one extent or another, for the rest of their lives.

John started running through some of the contingency plans he had made. He knew how to exit their property in Gulf Shores without detection. He knew the route from there to a simi public area. He knew where and how to borrow a car near their house. Perhaps he was just a little paranoid he thought.

He had made a few close friends since their relocation. But even in choosing these he had exercised caution. He befriended them but didn't really tell them much about their previous life in Texas. They were all people whom he had no real connection to. He valued distance when considering associations and friends. Anyone doing a background check would have a hard time connecting them. But, at the same time these were friends he could count on. Friends like Roy, back in Texas. Friends that had a physical rather than electronic connection to him.

As the two weeks progressed, John was surprised to find that he enjoyed learning all this spy stuff and he thought some of it could actually be useful. During the first week John had found a laundry area where he could wash his clothes. He had also started taking long walks around the base after dinner each evening. On these walks he reviewed the instruction that day and imagined how or where he might ever use such training. The last day they took an evaluation test. It was two-hundred multiple choice questions. This was used to evaluate the effectiveness of the classes. They also filled out a brief survey as to how they liked the classes. When the classes were over, John collected his luggage from the dorm room, was driven to the airport, and dropped off at the curb. The flight home was uneventful.

After landing in Mobile, Alabama, John got into his car and headed home. It was late Friday night when he finally got home. Even in the dim light, John could see the raised flower planter looked stunning. Rhonda had set it up perfectly. John would have to work watering the planter into his weekly schedule. Rhonda had also re-arranged the den while he was gone. As they kissed and John held Rhonda in his arms, he told her how good everything looked, especially her.

The next morning, he took a cup of coffee to a spot on the beach, near the surf. He didn't sit out on the beach much anymore. The novelty of it had soon worn off and he hated getting sand in his shoes and shorts. But when he really wanted to be alone with his thoughts, he left the deck and sat near the surf. The sound of the wind and waves would drown out everything else. Rhonda knew his thoughts were very far from the sand he sat on. She rarely intruded on his solitude when she saw him sitting alone on the beach. He never said so, but she could tell when he had some things to work out. She knew when she was a distraction and only hindered his figuring out whatever it was he was figuring out.

It had rained during the early morning hours and low clouds were still overhead. But the clouds broke up a little further out in the gulf and now the rays of sunshine were swiftly approaching the shore. The stiff cool breeze would have blown sand against his ankles if not for the recent rain. Sitting close to the roaring of the surf, looking out into the gulf, always made him think about how insignificant he was when compared to God's plan for the world and mankind. Just thinking about that seemed to make even his biggest problems seem small and insignificant. He weighed recent events and tryed to discern a prominent path. Was he being guided to something new or were these just random events to derail his current path? Was there a lesson to be learned? It was a lot to consider. He wondered what events the day might bring as he sat on the beach. He had an odd feeling of expectancy. Like something was about to happen. He had no clear expectations. But he had a feeling of anticipation that had stuck with him ever since the flight home. Was he imagining things or was he being prepared for a major change? He didn't have to wait long for an answer.

Rhonda called from the deck, waving the cordless house phone over her head. John couldn't hear what she was saying. But it appeared to be urgent. John poured his coffee out and ran up the back stairs. The resulting phone call was brief. After a quick visit to his home office, John returned to eat a late breakfast with Rhonda. She had made them some canned biscuits and chocolate gravy. After waiting as long as she could stand it, she asked "Well, what's up with the early phone call?"

"They want me to fly to Houston Monday morning."

"So soon? You just got home."

"Sorry. They didn't really give me a choice."

"But we were going to have Brent and Donna Jones over for dinner Monday night."

"I know. See if we can reschedule it for Thursday or Friday night."

"I'll call them later and see. What should I tell them."

"The truth. Tell them I got called away on business."

They were enjoying their breakfast. There was more John needed to share with Rhonda. But it could wait till after breakfast. Two minutes later the phone rang in John's study. It was Mike.

"Hi John. How's it going?"

"Fine, if I ever get to finish my breakfast. What's up Mike?"

"A friend tells me you're going to have to make a major decision soon."

"Oh really? A decision about what?"

"Yep. They got a hot one and need you on it like yesterday."

"I got the call from Houston already. How is this one different than the others?"

"My friend says you'll get an operations package tonight."

"There sending me the paperwork tonight on something I'll be in Houston for on Monday? Mike, I smell something that stinks! What's this all about?"

"I can't say for sure. But last time I checked, contractors don't take field training classes."

"The field training classes? But that was just..." John caught himself. "Do I have any options left?"

"John, I honestly don't know. I was just giving you a heads up."

"Mike, you know where I draw the line on this cloak and dagger stuff."

"Don't blame me. I've been out of the loop for almost a whole year now. I'll be retiring soon."

"Is there anything else you can tell me?"

"Not really. I just heard you got something that they need in the field on this one."

"What would you do?"

"I think it will come to you. They might just want you to train a field agent on computers or something. It might not be anything to worry about. But I'd still pray, really hard."

"For what?"

"I usually start with prayers for protection, guidance, and grace. You know that sort of stuff."

"Mike, you've come a long way since we first met."

"I had a pretty good push up that hill, as I recall."

"Thanks for the info, Mike. It means a lot to me to have a friend like you. I wish we lived a little closer."

"Be careful what you wish for."

"What do you mean by that? This is getting worse by the minute!"

"Nothing buddy. Just jerking your chain. Don't worry. You'll do the right thing. That's one thing I know for sure. I'll let you know if I hear anything else."

"Well, thanks for the call, I think. I need to get back to breakfast. Tell Lucy and the girls we said hi."

"Will do. Tell Rhonda the same. Goodbye."

After they finished cleaning up the breakfast dishes, Rhonda started washing clothes for John's trip. John went back out on the deck to focus his thoughts on what might transpire in Houston. planning for the worst and hoping for the best of outcomes. In the end he decided that he lacked enough information to formulate any ideas about what may or may not happen in Houston.

Rhonda came out to the deck to join him.

"Why are you going to Houston and what was that phone call about?"

"I'm not sure. Mike says it has something to do with the training classes they had me take."

"Anything else?"

"He says I'm going to have to make a decision soon. Not sure what he meant by that."

"That sounds ominous."

"Could be good or could be bad. No way of telling until I get there."

They both sat in silence wondering how many more opportunities they would have to enjoy this view. It seemed to them both that things were perhaps no longer calming down. They sensed a storm on the horizon of their lives. The Lord was moving their world again.

Later that evening, the doorbell rang. It was a courier with a delivery. John signed for the package and watched the plain white van leave the driveway. It was a sealed envelope with a memory stick inside. There were no instructions, no labels, no notes, nothing. John studied the courier's receipt. The delivery was via a private courier company he hadn't heard of. The receipt said the package was from the Houston office. John went to his home office and closed the door. Any other time he would have suspected the memory stick was from one of the CIA computer guys, trying to goad him into running a destructive program on his computer. But this had to be the "package" Mike had mentioned. John made a fresh backup of his computer system, unplugged the network connection and external disk drives and shoved the memory stick into the computer. The guys in Houston had encrypted the files and installed an auto cypher on the boot sector of the disk. The program prompted John to enter his CIA logon ID. John entered his ID and password. As the program displayed the first page of the file, John knew what it was. He had seen copies of operational case files many times before. However, until now, they had never given him a look at the file before he got to Houston. Why start sending him the files now? John began digesting the text on his screen. Perhaps the answer was in the files.

John read through the entire case files twice. The program lacked a print feature. This effectively prevented copying the text into other applications, such as a word processor. So John used a screen capture utility to copy and store a picture of the displayed data. He noticed the activity light on the memory stick when he closed the program. John thought it was a nice touch and a pretty slick trick. The reader program had erased all the data on the memory stick when the program was closed. The data was intended to be read only and read only once. John spent the next two hours running a text recognition program on the screen images he had stored. He put everything back into an electronic document format and copied the files to the memory stick they had sent to him. He would show those CIA computer geeks a thing or two. But that would have to wait until later.

There was something in the file that bothered him. One of the players was a guy named Peter Garrison. He seemed like he was just your normal guy. Except he appeared to have a loose association with a certain William Gates.

As a contractor for various government projects, Peter Garrison had access to some highly sensitive classified documents. Some of these went missing when Mr. Garrison was on campus working. The intel suggested that he might have sold them to William Gates. William Gates was a world-wide information broker. While never being convicted of anything the intel was fairly solid on him selling information to the highest bidder.

John reviewed the info on the players (as Mike liked to call them) and considered the facts. The suspect had an opportunity. Money might have been a motive. That could be easily checked. There was nothing to indicate Mr. Garrison had been coerced. He didn't have any past problems with gambling, debt, women, drinking or drugs. These were all the usual pressure points used to manipulate someone.

The association between the suspect and information broker was vague and sketchy. There was no firm data to suggest they actually knew each other or ever met. The intel really didn't prove anything. This case was thin.

John started laying out a rough plan of attack:

The objectives were:

1. Investigate financials.
2. Dig deeper into associations.
3. Approach the suspect for help/interview.
4. Approach the information broker for help/interview.

Goals:

1. Locate the files.
2. Recover documents.

3. Determine who has copies of the files.

Monday morning the early sky was tinted with brilliant red, orange, and yellow colors as John drove to Mobile, Alabama. He caught the first flight out to Houston. There was something majestic about seeing the sun rise from 30,000 feet. Once they landed, he picked up a rental car and headed into the city. It had been a while since he was in the downtown area. There had been lots of changes since then. But the road construction seemed to always be there, bottle-necking traffic, causing delays. In the entire eighteen plus years they had lived just North of Houston, John could not remember a time when they weren't working on most of the major roads. Sudden lane closures and detours were a way of life in the congested traffic in and around Houston.

After finding a place for the rental car in the parking deck, John found his way to the ninth-floor conference room and poured a cup of coffee. He was the first to arrive. He didn't have to wait long before the others started to drift in. Finally, John saw a familiar face; it was Mike. After making sure everyone was there, Mike closed the conference room door. He shook everyone's hand as he made his way to a seat. Mike introduced each of the team members by name and area of expertise. John was expectantly waiting to hear just what his area of expertise was. But Mike skipped John as he went around the table. Mike introduced himself and stated his role would be oversight of the operation and then he introduced John as the team lead for the operation.

John had led teams of developers on large programming projects while working for the utility company. But that was in his field of expertise. He had no idea what should happen next.

Mike saw John's 'deer in the head lights' moment. It was rare to see John stunned. Mike said to the team "Now that we know who's who I'm sure your team lead will want to hear your assessment of the material in your packets."

John went around the table giving each team member time to report their assessment and impressions of the operation. Fortunately, someone thought it would be best to assign only very experienced people to John's first assignment as team lead. There were a few suggestions of ways to pressure the players into cooperating and one team member mentioned it would be most efficient to just skip an investigation and interrogate the players. Normally, in this business, 'interrogate' did not mean a friendly chat. It meant physical persuasion and/or drugs to enhance the subject's willingness to be forthcoming. John considered these methods as non-options, or at most a last resort only.

John called for a fifteen-minute break while he made some notes. Part of being a team lead meant you had to type up a report on all meetings. When everyone returned and the door was shut, John started with the assignments.

1. Financial forensics on the players
2. Review and expand the background information on each of the players (Family, extended family, clubs, habits, preferences, health records, job, etc.). See if we missed anything.
3. Verify or eliminate the existence of any association between the players. Do they really know each other? Did they really meet? Do they have any history?

This would be a lot of work for their six-man team. It would take some time.

John finished the assignments and said "Under no circumstances does anyone contact the players, the players family, or friends. We want to have all our ducks in a row before they know we're investigating them. Any questions?"

There were none. John set their next team meeting in two weeks, on Monday, and the meeting was adjourned. It was 10:00.

John found an office he could use to type his meeting report. Thirty minutes later, Mike knocked on the door frame.

John looked up from his computer screen and saw Mike standing in the doorway.

"Well, how did I do Mr. Boss man?"

"I'm not your boss. You did great in there, for your first rodeo. I did have one suggestion. You might want to appear a little more supportive of the suggestions the team made. You don't have to like them or even use them. Just let them know you value their opinions. They are great assets to you. Understand?"

"You're right, of course. I'm just not comfortable with making any decisions that include interrogating people. A little pressure or manipulation here and there, if needed, I can see. But, that physical stuff, I don't know...."

"Don't worry my friend. That's exactly the reason they want you in the loop on certain cases. You get stellar results with a scalpel where we old school guys only know how to use a sledgehammer. Want to get some lunch?"

"Sure, give me an hour to finish up this report. Who do I send it to anyway?"

"Send it to me, I'll forward it on."

"OK, Mr. Boss man."

Mike shook his head. "I'll be back in an hour."

Mike swung by and picked John up at 11:30. They went to the parking deck and left for lunch at a restaurant called "Saltgrass". As they entered the hostess seated them at a table. Mike had never been a fan of dining in a booth. He always felt pinned in and a booth obstructed his view of the room. After being seated, Mike suggested that John try the "Range Rattlers" appetizer. John ordered the Range Rattlers and a Grilled Chicken Salad. Mike ordered the Fillet Mignon and a salad. As they sipped their iced tea and waited for their food, they talked about other people at the agency. Mike told John about some of his more interesting field operations projects. Nothing specific, just mainly how things had taken a surprising and sometimes funny turn in several of the operations he had been on. John listened intently. He was still trying to figure out where Mike's moral compass was. John asked Mike a few questions here and there for clarification. But mostly he just let Mike talk.

Mike suddenly realized he was carrying the conversation and telling John things he normally wouldn't have told anyone else. What was it about this guy that made you want to unload your world on him? Thankfully the food arrived, and he could keep his mouth shut while he had food in it.

After a delicious lunch, they drove back to the office. Mike had read John's meeting report and offered a few suggestions. John made the changes and emailed the corrected report to Mike.

John swung by Mike's desk and checked to make sure he could fly home that afternoon. It was already 1:30 and he had booked a 2:40 flight back to Mobile. Mike had no objections to him leaving. John placed a memory stick on Mike's desk. Mike said, "What's this?"

"I was hoping you might help me with something I've been working on. It's a simple communication program. If it works, we can send files back and forth in a secure fashion. I need someone to help with the testing. There is a password written on the side of the memory stick. You will need it for the test. You should probably only run it on your home PC. The computer geeks around here are very protective of the computers in this place. They would scream bloody murder if they found out you ran a rogue program on their network."

Mike shoved the memory stick in his pocket.

John continued, "I'll send you an email with an attachment tonight. Call me when you get it and I'll step you through the testing."

The flight back to Mobile was uneventful. It had been a long day and he was tired. John was glad he wouldn't have to think about the operation for a few weeks. As team lead, he knew he needed to do much better at encouraging his team members. But to be fair, they gave him zero warning that he was going to be thrown into the lead role.

In Mobile, John retrieved his car from the airport's long-term parking area and headed back to Gulf Shores. It would be close to seven when he got home. The rush hour traffic was already starting to build. John decided to stop at a florist shop on the way home. It had been a while since he had bought flowers for Rhonda, and he liked to surprise her every now and then.

When John got home, he gave Rhonda a stunning bouquet of red roses and hugged her.

"What's the special occasion?"

"Being home with you is always special for me. I sure did miss you."

"Just don't tell me we're having to move again. Did you eat on the way home?"

"No and No."

"I'll fix us a little something to tide us over until the morning."

John went upstairs to unpack his duffel bag while Rhonda made them some grilled cheese sandwiches. He had taken a few changes of clothes because he didn't know how long he was going to be in Houston. Lucky for him, it ended-up being a day trip. He always slept better in his own bed.

John gave Rhonda a kiss on the cheek as they sat down to eat. The grill cheese name was a bit of a misnomer. As he took a bite John could taste the thin slice of ham, Italian seasoning, and pepperoni on the grill cheese sandwich. Rhonda called them 'grill cheese dressed proper sandwiches' and they were delicious.

As they ate John told her about his trip, how he was all of a sudden the team lead, and what that meant. After they finished eating, John went to his office. He fired up his laptop and typed Mike a letter, thanking him for lunch and explaining the capabilities of the program he had placed on the memory stick. After the letter was finished, John ran his encryption program with the password he had given Mike. He attached the resulting encrypted file to a brief email asking Mike to call him when he got the email. In a few minutes John's cell phone rang. It was Mike.

John had Mike save the email attachment to his computer, open the file, look at the nonsensical jumble of letters and numbers, and close the file. Then he had him run the program on the memory stick. At the prompts Mike selected the file name and entered the password. Then John had him open the file again. This time he could read John's message.

John had him add a few lines to the bottom of the note and save the file. Then he ran John's program again, selecting the same file (now altered) and using the password. After the program ran, he opened the file, and it was once again scrambled into a nonsensical jumble of letters and numbers. John had Mike reply to his original email with the altered and encrypted file as an attachment. In a few minutes John read the lines Mike had added to the file.

It was a simple exercise. But it was a critical piece in a complete solution. This encryption could be used as a "stand alone" or incorporated into email systems, word processors, spreadsheets, anything. John needed some real cryptology pros to verify his encryption was good before he invested any more time in the project.

John thanked Mike and signed off for the night.

Thursday night, John and Rhonda went out to eat with Brent and Donna Jones. John and Brent had been friends since junior high school. Brent had been John's best man at their wedding. He was an accountant at a local manufacturing plant. Donna was a third grade school teacher. They met for dinner at a restaurant called John Barleycorn's.

John Barleycorn's was a trendy place built with amazing detail to decor. The ceilings were invisible in the subdued lighting because they were painted flat black and dotted with tiny lights that looked like stars. The table lighting was provided by a miniature floodlight that seemed to float over the table on an incredibly thin black wire. In the middle of the main dining area there was this funny structure with bits of this and that all over it. It was one of those things that made you look at it and wonder what it was ever used for.

As they entered, someone was being served a fajita platter. The sizzling meat and vegetables smelled amazingly good. But, after seeing the menu, they all had the filet mignon, baked potato, and salad. After they ordered Brent asked John, "So what happened to Monday night?"

"Sorry about that. I got called away on business at the last minute and couldn't get out of it."

"Sounds like the utility business may be more exciting than I thought."

"Not really. I just build and modify applications to meet the ever-changing utility business needs."

"A new way to get power to my house?"

"No. Nothing like that. It's more like new ways to forecast and meet growth demands. I do a lot of software integration between new programs they buy and existing reporting systems. So, how are things at your office."

Brent had known John long enough to tell when he was ducking a subject. Brent said, "Just counting the same beans over and over." They both laughed.

Brent asked John why they left Houston.

"Well, it got pretty crazy after I published the Prophet X program."

"Man, I forgot about that. What do you mean crazy?"

"Crazy people trying to find us. Just weirdos."

"Why didn't you market that program? It sounded like you could have made a bunch of money from it."

"There were people trying to steal the program. Bad people. The kind of people who you don't want looking for you."

"Man, that's crazy."

"Yep. It was a bad experience for us. There were more than a few times that I really regretted writing that Prophet X program. So, we ended up moving down here to start over. Sort of a new beginning for us."

"But you still got to keep your job at the utility company right?"

"Yes. They let me work from home mostly."

"Wow! That's incredible."

"So, how long have you and Donna been in Gulf Shores?"

"About twelve years. We jumped at the chance to move down here. We couldn't afford a house on the beach, like you. But, we've loved it here ever since we moved down from Arkansas."

After they finished dinner, they vowed to get together again soon, said goodnight, and went to their cars.

Two weeks later, John was back in Houston for the second team meeting. He let all the team members give their reports. The investigation results were:

An extensive financial forensics investigation of Peter Garrison revealed no large deposits, no hidden or offshore accounts, no major purchases, and no extraordinary debt. The enhanced background checks turned up no further information or actionable leads. The association between Peter Garrison and William Gates was based on the fact that they both were in Boston at the same time and both ate at a particular restaurant on the same night. One other coincidence, they both attended Virginia Tech, but at different times. Very circumstantial.

The team decided to interview Peter Garrison and see if he might willingly give them any further information.

Two of the team members arranged to meet with Peter Garrison and question him over lunch. As a government contractor he was very cooperative. He didn't understand why they were questioning him. But that was OK. He knew the government investigated everything.

The recommendation from the interview with Mr. Garrison was that he most likely did not know William Gates and had never met William Gates. While he technically had access to the stolen documents, there was no reason for him to check them out. Indeed, records indicated that he never requested the missing documents. With no further leads the team was at a dead end. The case would be shelved until new information became available.

John took a late flight back to Mobile. It would be almost midnight before he would get home. Being in Houston seemed to make John not feel afraid, just uneasy. He figured it must be because when they had lived there, people had actually tried to kill them. No way he could have ever figured anyone would want to kill or even harm him or his family.

But the Lord had protected him and his family then and he figured the Lord would continue to do so.

Chapter 2

~

Bill was working the night shift again. He worked in the Echelon office. Echelon was the name for an international telecommunications surveillance project that is carried out by a United Kingdom and United States alliance. The project monitored all electronic transmissions around the world. Their main feeds were from cellular towers and the internet these days. However, they also covered the radio frequencies and satellite phone communications. Any encrypted data was automatically sent through the new encryption AI (Artificial Intelligence) interface. It could decrypt most burst transmissions and almost all internet traffic that was encrypted. Since they brought the AI interface online, they rarely ever sent encrypted data off-site.

Bill saw the traffic hit the Encryption folder. Not unheard of but unusual. He followed procedures and forwarded the emails between John Davidson and Mike Lambert to the NSA (National Security Administration) offices for further analysis. While terrorist and drug cartels tended to use coded transmissions and sometimes encrypted them, they were always somewhat readable after the cyber geeks got done working their magic on it.

The NSA had their crypto code analysis team look at the messages. Most of the time if the AI couldn't break it, then there was little chance the crypto guys could do much with it. But those guys sure did love their word puzzles. After several weeks of analysis, they finally determined that it contained a new type of encryption scheme that was currently unknown and thus unbreakable using known methods. This caused the NSA to send a case file to the CIA for investigation and mandatory report back to the N.S.A.. Someone was going to have a great day explaining these messages to some not so friendly investigators.

Thursday Morning Mike Lambert received a call from McGuire, Director of CIA operations. He needed a chat a.s.a.p.. That normally indicated trouble. Mike left his full cup of coffee on his desk as he headed for McGuires office. McGuire asked him to close the door. Not a good sign. McGuire shoved the NSA report to Mike. Mike skimmed the report. Oh no! John had gotten them flagged.

Mike asked, "What do we need to do to fix this?"

"What was in the encrypted files?"

"It was just a test. No real content worth anything. He briefly told me what his program did and how to add a little to the file and encrypt it before sending it back to him. We were just testing his program. That's all."

McGuire replied, "My guess is that John will have to give them his source code and perhaps explain it to them. They're not programmers; they're code breakers. Those young bucks just use the tools us old farts built for them. Pretty good chance John created some off the wall code that they've never seen before. He'll probably have to explain it to them."

Mike went back to his office and phoned John. He told John what was going on.

John said, "Mike, why is it every time I write a program the government thinks they have the right to take it from me? Are they just picking on me or what?"

Mike let John blowoff a little steam and then asked John a question, "John, do you think you should be compensated for your program?"

John thought for a minute, "Absolutely! I developed it. I spent hours creating it. I should get compensated."

"There you go. You said the program was incomplete as is. I think you mentioned email program, word processing and spreadsheet integration; or something like that. Well, I'm not sure, but I suspect the government will pay a whole lot for it just as is. Think about it."

Suddenly, John wasn't quite as upset as he was a minute ago. "Thanks Mike. I needed a touch of reality. I guess I just really don't like people taking my stuff without saying 'please'. Tell them boys, to come ask me real nice." And he laughed.

He thanked Mike again and they ended the call.

It didn't take long. The next morning McGuire called John in to Houston for lunch meeting the following Thursday.

In McGuire's office he was meeting with Robert Saunders the Director of Cryptography for NSA. They were meeting to discuss John's encryption program. McGuire asked Robert if he'd heard anything about John Davidson. Robert replied he had read the Prophet X reports.

McGuire asked, "Why do you think we brought him in on our team?"

"I suspect you needed something from him that wasn't in the reports."

"In a way, you are correct. Have you ever met someone who is so different in their thinking that you can't figure out how they come up with ideas? That's John. He doesn't think like you or me or anyone else we've ever met. He has a moral and ethical code that we've only heard about in Sunday School when we were kids. But that's just the base of John. His biggest asset is that he thrives outside the box. He doesn't know it, but he loves making it up as he goes and inventing different ways to accomplish things few can. He's smart and he prefers living outside the norm where he makes the rules and he's in control. If you try to box him in, you'll find him to be just a vapor. As you no doubt read in the Prophet X files, he ran circles around our best experienced field people and around some of our best computer experts."

Mike could see Robert Saunders was not convinced (yet).

"I'm fixing to give you some advice. You're not going to give it much credence. But if you don't you will wish you did as sure as the sun comes up tomorrow. Be fair and respect John for who he is and what he has accomplished. He developed a cryptography program that you, all the fancy degrees in your department, and your cutting-edge computers can't crack. He has no degree of any sort. Consider that for a moment and tell me that doesn't make him special. Imagine what he could do if he actually worked with your department. Robert, you do whatever you want with John. Just don't underestimate him. If you do, then it will cost you in ways you can't even dream of."

McGuire gave Robert the location and time of the lunch meeting the following day and ended the meeting.

John was 20 minutes early getting to the restaurant. He had purchased a small digital recorder. It easily fit in his shirt pocket, and it was voice activated. In his test it performed well. Shortly, McGuire and another man came to the table.

McGuire introduced Robert as Director of cryptography for the NSA. They ordered their drinks and John decided to dive right into it.

"Mr. Saunders, where do you call home?"

"I live on the airbase at Langley."

"I see your wedding ring. Been married long?"

"It will be thirteen years in June?"

"Congratulations. Children?"

"We have two boys."

"Wow! I bet that's a challenge for the wife?"

"She keeps them in line."

"Did you two meet in the air force?"

"No, I was assigned to Norfolk Naval Air Station, and she was working for a local car dealer and I bought a new car from her."

"So, she talked you into buying a new car and then she talked you into marriage?"

"Now that you mention it..." they laughed.

"Mr. Saunders, I guess I'll find out sooner or later. But why did you want to meet me?"

Robert was hoping to build a little rapport before getting into the specifics. But it looked like that wasn't going to happen. So be it.

"John, we've got some text files you sent to Mike Lambert that are very interesting to us. I was hoping to ask you about them."

"Reading peoples mail, are we? Well, I can see where these messages might have drawn your attention. Sorry for any problems I may have caused your department. But I'm not sure exactly what convinced you these were just text messages. It's not likely that you've already discovered a way to crack my encryption, or we wouldn't be here. I suspect that you've likely been talking to Mike Lambert."

Through John's intense, wide-open, hazel eyes, Robert could see the gears in John's mind spinning at warp speed. Robert was starting to remember what McGuire had said about John. He was also starting to wonder how many moves ahead of this discussion John was.

"Thank you for your understanding of the situation. Could I ask what was in the messages?"

"Nothing sinister I can assure you. I was testing a new communication protocol that I have been developing and Mr. Lambert was kind enough to send me a short message back after receiving my original message. Does that help?"

"Well, yes and no. To be quite frank, we would like to know what software you used to encrypt the messages. It does not seem to conform to any known cryptographic systems."

"Interesting. It does not conform to any known encryption systems because it is my own design. Am I to understand that you could not decrypt my messages?"

"John, given sufficient time and text we can decrypt most anything. However, it would save a lot of time and resources if you would simply tell us how you encrypted the messages."

"I could explain it to you. But, I do not have the education your guys do and it would be like a hunter trying to explain to a surgeon how he sowed someone's guts back in. It would be much better to just show it to your guys. Do you think your team would benefit from studying the program I wrote, the source code?

"Certainly, would you be willing to make that available to us?"

"Absolutely! But I've spent a lot of time developing the code. I didn't have a college degree in cryptography to help me. So, I had to learn it on my own, by studying and trying to understand all the cryptography math and methods I read about. And I don't have a math degree either. A lot of that stuff just didn't make since to me. Anyway, I do enjoy learning. I spent a lot of time developing this program. I'm thinking I should be somewhat compensated for my time and hard work. If your guys can not break my code with your crypto degrees and AI crypto computer, then I figure I must have done a pretty good job. Besides If you guys can't read it, then I bet no one else can either. It could be a great asset to our government for coded transmissions. Does that sound like an accurate assessment to you?"

"Go on."

"I'm thinking a hack proof encryption scheme would be a great asset for the government. Your team could take my code, adapt it to meet the government's needs and deploy it. That would really earn your team some kudos. Something like that has to be worth a little money. So, Yes, I do have an offer for you."

Robert had to admit, this was starting to sound like an enticing proposition. "Please continue."

"I will give you a week explaining the code and methods I used to create my encryption system to your team. I will train them in how to build their own encryption schemes based on my code. I'll give you the working prototype and source code. All I ask for in return are two things. First, my name is never associated with or included in reports of the new encryption system your team will develop from this. Second, I will need a small monetary compensation for my time."

"What compensation did you have in mind?"

"1.2 million US dollars."

"John, That's not going to happen."

"OK, Then, make me an offer. Surely my time and work is worth something." Now they were negotiating. John was relieved this seemed to be working as he had planned. The downside to John's proposition was that a case could easily be made to imply he was threatening to sell the software to someone else. That would be very bad for John and cheaper for the government.

Robert thought for a moment. He had been expertly maneuvered into a sales pitch that made this sound like a win-win deal. Robert offered, "Seven hundred and fifty thousand and a week of your time." They had paid more for contractors to develop new software before.

John countered, "Let's make it an even million, with the week of my time, and call it a day. You know it's worth it and more."

Robert was thinking about his options. He could just have the CIA take the code by brute force and save a lot of money. But, they might spend years trying to understand his source code. Then, he considered that little chat with McGuire and the program must be pretty sophisticated to pass their AI cypher analysis. They really needed John to explain how it worked.

"It's a deal. I'll expect you in Langley, Virginia next week, with the code and a whole lot of question and answer time with my guys."

"I'll be there. I will need some plane tickets, a hotel, and an address."

"McGuire will arrange your travel. I'll have someone from my office pick you up at the airport."

They ordered lunch and only then did Robert get to visit with and learn what made John different. John was open to discussing how he developed the Prophet X program, all his exploits in Europe and what was important to him. Lunch was over before they knew it. But more than that, what intrigued Robert as well as the rest of the people in the CIA was that John reminded them of some things they had once aspired to obtain, truthfulness, honesty, integrity, righteousness. The job had long since required too many compromises in all these areas and more. John reminded all of them of this. Robert was hoping to spend more time with John in Langley. Perhaps at lunch. There was something that made you want to spend more time with John. It was true, he seemed to think differently than most folks. It was hard to put his finger on it. But Robert liked having this guy around. He was a rogue element in their otherwise neatly organized, categorized, predictable world.

Once in the car and on the way to the airport, McGuire ask Robert, "what do you think of Mr. Davidson?"

"He's different."

"Yes, he has that effect on most of us."

"Mike, the NSA has a special think tank for people like John. I've met a few of those guys. They primarily work on counterintelligence scenarios, spy games if you will. They are trained and practice thinking three moves ahead. I think that's what John is."

"Robert, you only know about John, what John wanted you to know. You didn't realize it, but you gave him a lot to work with."

"How so?"

"Why do you suppose he asked you all those questions about your family?"

"Uh, I guess he was just being polite."

"No. John was gathering information on you. You gave him plenty to work with. He doesn't do things just because it's nice or expected. But, he always takes precautions and stacks the cards. If there is even a chance that there will ever be a game to play, he's already got all of the aces before the first card hits the table. He also has other unique facets to his character. He's honest, loyal, and trustworthy. If he tells you he will do something, then you can bet the farm, if there is any way in the world to make it happen, then John will get it done. He expects the same honesty from others."

"I see."

"No, you can only truly appreciate and understand the uniqueness of John when you see him in action. For most folks, it's way too late when they finally figure out something is happening. I'm only telling you this to try and convince you to play it straight with John. Be honest with him and he will be an asset to you. Try to take advantage of him, and, well, you've read his file, use your imagination."

John arrived at the Ronald Reagan Washington National Airport, Monday morning at 9:45. There was a guy at baggage claim with a sign that read "J. Davidson". After confirming who John was, the guy didn't say much during the 25-minute ride to the Langley Airforce Base. Once there, John was escorted to a security building where he received a visitor's badge. Next, his escort took him to a non-descript building on the far side of the base. Once inside he was given directions to a conference room. When he entered, there were two guys working on their laptops. They introduced themselves and informed John the rest of the team would be there shortly.

After everyone arrived Robert Saunders introduced everyone. John had sent them all of his source code and program files, by government currier, on a memory stick, several days earlier. He had hoped that these guys could quickly make sense of his code and didn't have many questions. This was wishful thinking as it turned out.

After a few questions it became apparent for this to work John was going to have to teach, as best he could, the methods and functions he had used in the cryptography program. John said "I have a suggestion. I think this would go a lot quicker if I could just use the whiteboard, step through the program, and try to explain the code as I go. Afterwards, you guys can ask questions. What do you think?"

Everyone was nodding affirmative. So, John began. This was just like the many times he had described applications that he had proposed to solve operational process problems at the utility company. But this time he was explaining it to kindred minds, programmers. He covered the modules in his encryption program, their function, inputs, and outputs.

To their credit the team was very studious and taking notes as John spoke. John had filled the whiteboard with a high level overview of all the encryption modules in his program. He explained how each module worked by referring to the printed copy of the source code.

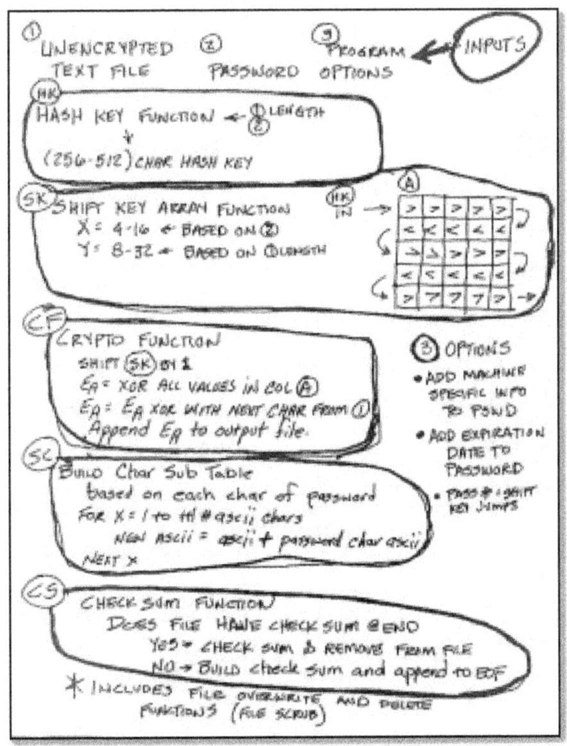

It took him about 4 hours to cover all the nuts and bolts of the program. When he finished the team seemed unusually quiet. So, John asked, "Any questions?". Everyone looked around the table to see who would go first. This was going to take a while.

Robert took John to lunch. While they were eating, it occurred to John that Robert hadn't said much. "What do you think? Are you guys getting your money's worth yet?"

Robert didn't say anything for a while, as he chewed his food. "Can I ask you a question?"

"Sure, we're all friends now. Right?"

"How did you come up with all this stuff? Why did you get interested in cryptography? And how in the world did you learn to code like that? Half my team hasn't got a clue what you're talking about and the other half is trying to soak it up as fast as they can."

"Wow, I don't know where to start. Maybe you need to hire smarter guys. You know, ones without degrees." John was grinning. "Look, I'm not crazy brilliant. I just thought of a different way to arrange standard crypto functions to jumble up the text in a way that your guys have never seen before."

"Close. But not exactly. I'll tell you what my team will not. I think you misunderstood most of the encryption functions you used. You modified them to make sense to you. They aren't in any papers or labs or anywhere. You actually created new functions that do things in a most unusual way. That's PHD level stuff or dumb luck. At any rate my team is jealous as heck that they didn't think of it. In one day you've given them more new ideas about encryption than they got in a semester at MIT."

"Robert, do you think they understand me? I mean I'm explaining it as best I can. I can dumb it down to compensate for their degrees if you think it will help." John was full of it and grinning from ear-to-ear.

"Out of the six guys listening to you. I have two that are soaking it up. The rest are struggling with most of your functions because they are non-standard. Just let them work through it. They'll get it and once they do. We'll put these new encryption methods to good use."

They finished their lunch and headed back to the Air Base.

The rest of the week went by pretty fast. John enjoyed working with the team. By the end of the week John and the team were working on ways to package the new encryption functions and add them to an email system. Once the guys had his methods down, they added some additional subroutines to enhance the encryption strength further.

Towards the end of the week, Robert took John aside and had him sign a non-disclosure agreement. It seemed the government now knew how his encryption program worked and they didn't want anyone else to know about it. The agreement guaranteed a one-million-dollar payment to John for exclusive rights to the source code and program. It prevented him from disclosing or building anything that was similar to his original program. Losing the program, his baby, stung a little bit, but that one-million-dollar check would make all that go away. Funny thing, the government gave him a million and then the IRS took a chunk of it back. Still a nice pay day.

As he got on the plane headed home, John was somewhat sad to see the week come to an end. He and the team were making great strides. John was learning from them, and they were learning from him. It was great to work with people who understood your thought process. Well, sort of. He and the team had gotten 90% of the email encryption project completed. It would have been great to see it rolled out. At any rate John would most likely not be able to play with data encryption ever again.

Chapter 3

~

John got to work from home for a few weeks. His 'vacation' from the utility company had caused the work requests to pile up. Mostly these were requests to add or change existing applications. This kept his mind off the week in Langley and kept him busy.

McGuire phoned and congratulated John on a job well done in Langley. It appeared that if he wished he could move from Operations to the work Encryption group in Langley. Apparently, the Encryption group had recently been awarded a generous budget increase for a new encryption project. John considered it for a few days and then declined. He wanted things to settle down for a while. He had Robert's phone number and email address should he change his mind later.

Two days later John had another package delivered by special currier. He made travel arrangements to be in the Houston office the following Monday.

On Monday, after reviewing all the data on the memory stick, John entered the conference room at the CIA's Houston office. He was relieved to see Mike Lambert's face in the room. Mike opened the meeting just as before. He introduced all the agents in the room and then introduced John as the team lead.

There was a missing witness in an ongoing FBI case. The CIA was lending a hand in tracking down the witness. With budget constraints, over the past few years, the FBI was always short on manpower. The CIA was happy to help in return for a few favors here and there.

The witness had gone missing the week before. There were few leads. However, there were several suspects. The primary suspect was:

Marshall Spencer – 38 years old, convicted drug dealer, incarcerated for 3 years and 2 months on possession, intent to deliver, evidence tampering and resisting arrest charges. Currently on parole. Several theft and assault convictions before that.

The information continued with his parole officers contact information, known addresses, associates and relatives; the sort of info needed for a proper hunting party.

The team prioritized the contacts they would make based on the relationship to the subject. Oddly enough, in many cases the family tended to cut ties with career violent offenders. The team opted for a hands-on approach. No phone calls. They would conduct face-to-face interviews. It was a little more time consuming, but it was difficult to read people over the phone. In person they tended to be a little more forthcoming and truthful. His team split-up the first round of interviews and set a meeting time for the following week.

John spent the next few hours typing up the meeting report and sending it to Mike Lambert. Then he enjoyed dinner with Mike and his family. The next morning he flew back to Mobile and drove home.

Thursday, John got a call from one of the team's investigators. They had located the suspect in a dilapidated trailer deep in the woods. It was one of the places the suspect was known to have had cooked meth in, a few years prior. The local sheriff's department had arrested him on possession, a felon in possession of a control substance, a felon in possession of a firearm and various other parole violations. He was going back to prison. John had the FBI request that one of his team interview the suspect before he was deported. In exchange for some leniency at sentencing, the suspect confessed to killing the witness and after some more promises he even told them where he buried the body.

The next evening John received a field report on the interview. The operation seemed to be concluding soon.

The following Monday, John's team met back in the same Houston conference room as the week before. Everyone had forwarded their field reports to John and reported their progress to the team. These would all have to be forwarded up the chain of command and ultimately to the FBI.

Before the operation was officially closed, the team had to have approval to close it. It didn't take long. Mike Lambert took John to lunch and informed him he could close the operation. John would submit a high-level summary report of what the team actually did and that was all there was to it.

On the flight from Houston to Mobile, John was reading one of the field reports. Something was nagging him. There was another suspect. A Mr. Thomas Tyler. He had numerous arrests and no convictions. Always around and in contact with that Marshall Spencer guy. He was also associated with half a dozen other career criminals. John hated leaving unanswered questions.

The following day he phoned the team member that had contacted and interviewed Thomas Tyler.

"Hello?"

"Hey Bill, this is John Davidson. Did I catch you at a bad time?"

"No, I was just heading into the gym. Desk work tends to make the gut grow if you know what I mean."

"Yep, I can relate. I could stand to lose a few pounds myself. Great job on the field work and report. I called because I wanted your impressions of the Thomas Tyler guy you interviewed."

"Well, my report covers all the facts. But this guy is smarter than your average criminal. I think he's got his hands in a lot of illegal stuff. But he keeps everything at arm's length. He never gets his hands dirty. We don't tell the FBI how to run their business. But if we did, we should tell them to investigate the heck out of that guy. He's a major player."

"Bill, thanks for your candor. That's exactly what I needed to know. I sort of suspected the same thing. Hey man, have a good work out and do a few reps for me, OK?"

"Will do. See you next Monday?"

"Maybe, I have to make a few calls first. Goodbye. Have a good day."

After he hung-up, John phoned Mike Lambert and told him what he had discovered."

"John, bad news. They've already closed the operation down."

"Mike what about this Thomas Tyler guy. What do we do about him?"

"Nothing, this is an FBI case; not our monkeys, not our circus."

"But Mike this could lead to some really big shakers and movers in the drug world."

"I repeat, not our monkeys, not our circus. It's a domestic thing. Were International, remember?"

"So, is there nothing we can do?"

Mike thought for a moment, "You still have to submit the high-level summary to close the operation. You might carefully word a specific and clear reference to Mr. Thomas Tyler. With any luck they will act on it later."

"Mike, can I come in and file my report Monday afternoon."

"Sure, you don't really have to come in to file your report. You can just send it through the normal secured channels. But if you want to file it in person, that'll be great by me. Lucy and the kids would love to have you over for dinner again."

"Sounds good. See you Monday."

John had phoned Luke Morgan and asked him about getting some time on the CIA's new AI (Artificial Intelligence) computer system. Luke wanted to know how John had heard about the new project. But, instead he just said he'd see what he could do. Luke made a few calls and then gave John a contact name and phone number.

By the time John's flight from Mobile landed at Bush Intercontinental Airport he had absorbed all the material he could about machine learning and the new open-source AI platforms. He wasn't sure how or if this might work out. But he would have fun learning if nothing else.

After arriving at the Houston CIA offices John was met by Ms. Ricky Roberts. Ricky was a brainiac and over the new AI lab. Ricky escorted John to a small room with several large server racks in the corner. She explained the hardware first. These were top of the line multi process servers with massive, raided solid state disk storage systems to store and manage huge volumes of data. There was a custom sub processor unit in it's own rack. It was specially designed and handled the real-world connection (internet). It handled intrusion detection and scanned all documents for viruses and malicious code before the AI servers could access them.

John asked Ricky about using the lab for a few hours. Ricky told him he had been cleared for it's use for the whole morning. With that Ricky showed John how to access the system and where the tools they had developed were located. John thanked her. He briefly asked her some questions about the system to make sure he understood how the tools worked before she left the room.

John investigated the AI tools they had developed first. There was no reason to reinvent the wheel if he didn't need to. One of them looked promising. He played with it for a while and then determined it needed a little help to do what he had in mind. This was going to take a while and he only had the room till 1pm.

John didn't leave the chair all morning. Focused on the code he was developing, testing, and modifying. A repetitive "Plan, Do, Check, and Adjust" cycle. But, eventually, if he had enough time, he'd get there. At 12:00 he figured it was as good as he'd have time to make it. He started his program and fed it the name: "Thomas Tyler," Mr. Tyler's birthday, and his last known address. He ran the program. It would take the program a few minutes to pull data from the FBI case, the field reports, the Internet, various arrest records, various county and state investigative reports, news agencies, banking records, etc... In theory this AI should be able to sort, cull and prioritize all this information about Mr. Tyler. It would return all his known associates and rank them by relevance. This included everything: where he bought groceries, gas stations he used, girlfriends he phoned, his attorneys, even his barber. Everywhere there was an electronic footprint for Mr. Tyler, the data was pulled into the search. It should give them a comprehensive look into Mr. Tyler's life. If it worked this would make it easy to see who, if anyone, was connected to Mr. Tyler's operation. There were a few things missing, but only because John didn't know how or have access to the data. It occurred to him google might have a tracking data on his cellular phone and then there was the Echelon groups data (emails, phone conversations). Man with those two data sources it would be easy for the AI program to do a very complete, in-depth, background check on someone without anyone ever lifting a finger.

This would be a huge leap in investigative power when it got dialed in.

In five minutes, the AI program spit out a 95 page report. John skimmed it and then emailed it to himself. He could digest it later. John phoned Ricky's extension and asked her to come in. In a few minutes Ricky was in the secure room with John. John showed her what he had developed and asked her if she wanted him to delete his code and return the system as he had found it. She said he should leave all his code changes on the system and told him they could back them out later if they needed to. John thanked her and left her in the secure AI computer lab.

The following week, Ricky had an impressive report on the changes John had made to their code. It showed a lot of interesting (unconventional) approaches to data gathering. John had sent her an email thanking her for the use of the AI lab and suggested they add google and Echelon data to enhance the AI search engine.

By 2pm he had spent an hour reviewing the AI report. He phoned McGuire and asked if he could come see him. McGuire told him to come to his office.

They shook hands and sat down at a small worktable in McGuire's office.

"John, let me guess. You have that summary report for me to review. Right?"

"Well, no. I still have a problem."

McGuire knew John could be a pain. All he needed was for John to file that summary report and easy breezey another case closed. Another favor done for the FBI. But suddenly McGuire had the nagging feeling he'd be needing that Excedrin bottle again before John let this case go.

"McGuire, how much do you know about the CIA's new AI computer lab?"

"Just that it's new and it's under the tech department's budget. Why, you want to do some work with them?"

"I got about four hours in their lab this morning."

"Did you break it or fix it?" Grinning

"No, they let me use it. I used it to run a deep background checked on Timothy Tyler."

"And you think we should use it to help with other cases?"

"Yes. But that's not it. Mr. Tyler is connected to a Mr. Samuel Zimmer. Does the name ring any bells?"

"It might, go on."

"Mr. Zimmer is indirectly connected to three other current CIA operations and six active FBI cases. He's the common thread, the shot caller, or whatever you spooks call them. He's at the root of all of these on-going investigations, plus his associates are connected to dozens of police incidents across the south."

McGuire thought for a moment. "Organized crime and racketeering are FBI's problem, not ours."

"Yes, I already got the 'not our monkeys, not our circus' speech from Mike Lambert. Don't you people even care?"

"John, things work slowly in the government. Especially when you're talking about cooperation between different branches of the government. It's all tit-for-tat., 'I'll give you this if you give me that'. John, like it or not, that's the official policy. Let's take a walk. It's such a pretty day and I need some fresh air."

Once they were out in the courtyard a block away, McGuire continued, "Unofficially, there are certainly people who care. These people talk at lunch and dinners. They maintain back channels of communication for certain situations. Situations that warrant going outside the official policy. They all know that by doing so they risk everything. If they get caught, they know they will lose their job, their career, and be prosecuted to the fullest extent possible. It's policy. Understand?"

"Yes."

"With that being said. There is a friend of mine in the State Department. He will get your information into the right hands. When you meet him don't mention my name. He will be expecting you. I'll set it up for tomorrow at lunch. Whatever this report is that you have you need to sanitize it. Don't leave anything in it that can be traced back to yourself or the CIA."

"But it's just a bunch of data from multiple sources that connects the dots."

"Listen, I don't want to know about it. You and I never discussed it. Period."

"Got it. How will I know who this guy is, where and when to meet him?"

"Mike will tell you. He will mention the guy's name in an unrelated conversation and then he will invite you to lunch at a specific restaurant at a specific time and mention his favorite table location. Tell Mike you're busy and can't make it. At lunch you go meet the guy. Got it?"

"Yes. Do I get a secret code word, a secret handshake, or a secret agent name?"

"Of course not. You watch too many movies."

Then McGuire noticed the grin on John's face.

"Laugh it up buddy. But, if you get caught passing information, you're not going to be laughing for a very long time. You better be sure this is worth the risk. It could very well end life as you currently know it."

"I'll be careful. Thanks for the help."

"John, one more thing. Once you pass the information, burn that report. No copies, no data files, no excerpts, nothing. And close that case today as soon as you get back to the office."

"Got it. Man, this would be so much easier if we could just talk to the FBI directly."

"It's not the government way. Politics, power, prestige, and all that garbage."

With that they returned to the office and John typed up his summary report while he waited for Mike to drop by the temporary office he normally used.

Around 4pm Mike popped into John's temporary office. "You free for dinner? Linda and the girls have been on my case for not inviting you over."

"Free as can be. Looks like I'll be here through tomorrow sometime."

"I still need to find a guy in the State Department named Robert Tillman and see if he has any questions for us, then we can go to the house whenever you're ready. How about lunch tomorrow, say 12:30? There's this restaurant called Luigi's, it's a super great Italian place. They have a table near the back and to the right as you go in. You can see the Houston skyline from there, it's very nice. So, how about it?"

"Wish I could. I already have plans for lunch tomorrow. Thanks anyway. Finish up your paperwork and come back when you're ready to go."

With that Mike left and John continued reading over the report from the AI labs program. He had trimmed all the non-critical data from the report. The FBI could find out who his barber was on their own if need be. He left plenty of meat for them, should they follow-up on the information.

By the time Mike came back, John had reduced it down to a 50-page report. Still a little fluff he could cut out. But that would have to wait until the morning.

After dinner and visiting with Mike's family, John returned to his hotel room. He was getting tired of being away from home so much. What had started out as an "every once in a while" thing, was now a day or two every week. John knew he would have to find a way off this ride soon.

At 12:30 John walked into Luigi's restaurant. The hostess asked him if he had a reservation. He told her he was there to meet a friend. He spotted a man sitting alone at a table in the right rear of the dining area. Most of the other tables in that area were empty.

John inquired, "Mr. Tillman?"

"Yes."

"John Davidson, may I join you?"

"Yes."

Tillman didn't say much and that made for an awkward few minutes. John couldn't get a read on this guy. After their food had arrived John told Mr. Tillman he had some information that needed to be acted on. Tillman asked what type of information. John told him it was evidence of an organized crime syndicate operating in the southern states and possibly spreading. Tillman considered this for a moment.

Then he simply said, "Give me your information. I'll make sure it gets into the right hands." John placed the large envelope and a $50 bill on the table, excused himself and left the restaurant. The food was good. But, John figured the less time he spent with Mr. Tillman, the better for all parties concerned.

Tillman left the money and envelope on the table while John left the restaurant. After John left, Tillman quietly ate his steak alone, considering what might be in the envelope and if he really wanted to touch it.

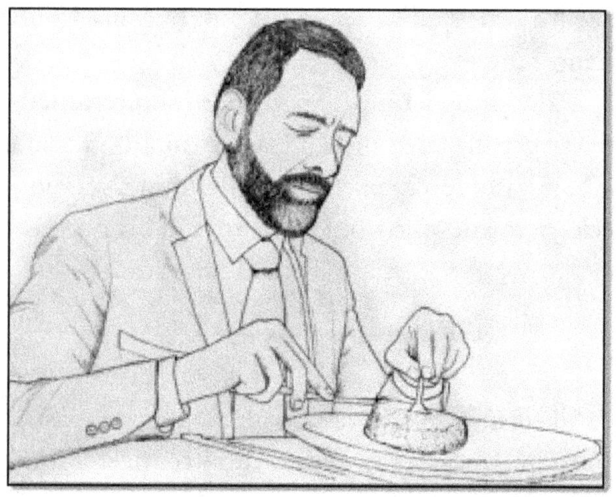

John returned to the CIA offices, sent his high-level summary report to Mike, said his goodbyes, and headed to the airport. He was halfway to Mobile before he decided what was done, was done. There was nothing more he could do about it. Time to quit thinking about it and move on.

John's work with the CIA was starting to draw unwanted attention. He was becoming known to the office folks at the Houston CIA offices. The use of the AI lab had drawn even more unwanted attention. Apparently, Ms. Ricky Roberts had blabbed to everyone about the code enhancements he had left on the new AI computer system. With all the attention, he was starting to feel like it was time to jump off this ship.

Staying around the CIA was going to bring trouble, sooner or later. It would soon be time to start planning for a graceful exit from the CIA. He figured he had more than repaid them for their help.

Chapter 4

~

John and Rhonda had continued their nightly walks around the neighborhood since moving to Gulf Shores. They had seen another couple walking in the neighborhood a few times. This time they took the opportunity to stop and meet the other couple. For some reason John immediately felt at ease while meeting the other couple. They lived just two blocks away from each other. The couple's names were Ron and Rita Porter. To John's surprise, Rhonda invited them over for ice cream. They all went to the Davidson's house. Over ice cream they found that they had many things in common. After they had left, John asked Rhonda why she had invited them over. Rhonda said she was tired of not having any close friends. She felt like eighteen months was long enough to live like hermits. John had to admit he was missing having close friends too.

The next day from his home office John sent Mike a request for information on the Porter's. Later that day, Mike sent him an email that had next to nothing in it. It showed the places they had lived and worked, schools attended, tax returns, driver's license, and birth certificates. Not much else was known without digging into their backgrounds. That would have raised a few red flags. They appeared to be clean and exactly who they said they were. John thanked Mike, deleted the email, and shredded the report.

Two days later, John was walking the neighborhood, trying to get some much-needed exercise. As he walked past the Porter's house, he saw Ron standing outside fixing a water sprinkler head. He stopped and visited with Ron for a few moments. John helped him replace the sprinkler head before finishing his walk and returning home.

Ron was accustomed to fixing things on his own. John's kind of guy. Over the next month John and Ron would cross paths on several occasions. Each time enjoying the encounter more as they got to know each other. After about a six weeks and a dozen visits, John came to a decision about the Porters. John told Rhonda his plan before proceeding. Rhonda agreed. They would not drive to the Porter's house or call them on the phone. The idea was to not leave an electronic connection between themselves and the Porter's.

A few days later, John invited the Porter's over for dinner. They had burgers, French fries, and cheese dip on the patio. It wasn't anything fancy, just an excuse to visit with their new friends. After they had finished the meal, John asked to speak with Ron alone. They went to the beach. John told him about Prophet X and that was why they had relocated to Gulf Shores. He told Ron what he did for the CIA. He didn't tell Ron everything, but enough to explain why people were after them. He asked if Ron had any questions. Thankfully Ron didn't know what to think and had no questions at the moment. Then, John got to the point.

"Ron, considering how things went in Texas, I need to always have a plan for getting out of here, should the need arise. I need a safe, secure route out of the neighborhood if someone shows up at the house unexpectedly. I was hoping you guys might be able to help in that regard. You wouldn't have to do anything. Just stay on the outside where no one can trace you back to us or more properly us to you. Have you noticed we have never called you on the phone or driven to your house?"

"I guess that's right. Why is that important?"

"We don't want our cars or phones traced to you guys in any way. Same with emails and cell phones. We don't carry them to your house, ever. That way there is no electronic trail between us. Understand?"

"Well, yes. I see what you mean. But why?"

"Should we need to leave. We will need to do it in a way no one can follow us. Working with the CIA I have seen firsthand how easy it is to track someone. We leave electronic tracks everywhere we go. Is that an android phone you have in your pocket?"

"Yes, why? Google tracks you wherever you take that phone. If you search around in Google, they will even show you all the data they keep on you. People can access that data and find out where you've been. But there are tons of other ways people can track you down electronically as well. The point is, not leaving an electronic trail gives us an out, just in case."

"So, you get to our house, then what?"

"First of all, it will never happen. But if it did, then we would need to leave the area, unobserved and undetected. We'd likely head towards Mobile or Panama City. They both have lots of people and it would be easy to blend in with all the tourists."

"How would you get there?"

"Well, a cab or Uber would leave an easy trail for someone to follow. I guess we might need to borrow one of your cars. We would leave a note and money to compensate you for the trouble. You guys could pick it up later. Look, this isn't a likely scenario at all. After all we've been through, I like to plan for all contingencies, even one as remote as this."

"I don't know. I'll need to discuss this with Rita first."

"Yes, please do. Wait till you guys get home. You can tell me what you guys decided next time I see you. Either way you guys decide is fine with us. We're not pressuring you to do anything. We are just so blessed to finally have some real friends. We've been keeping a very low profile for the better part of a year and a half. That has meant no close friends for a long time now. You and Rita are the only ones we have told. And Ron, no matter what you guys decide, please don't tell anyone else about us."

"I understand. Thanks for confiding in me."

After the Porter's went home, John told Rhonda what he had done. It felt good to let someone know what and who they really were. No more hiding like some criminals.

Several days later the doorbell rang. It was Ron. John invited him out on the rear deck. Ron said he and Rita had discussed it and agreed to help them. John thanked him and told him he would be by their house in a few days.

Later that week John stopped by and asked the Porters if he could store a padded envelope in their garage. John hid the package behind some paint cans. The envelope contained a memory stick with all his documentation. On it he had photos, names, taped recordings, meetings, places, dates, and times. It was all there along with their passports and some cash. While in the garage, the Porter's showed John where they kept spare keys for the cars. John thanked them and walked back to his house. If things went sideways this was their insurance package, their way out. It would let John put some distance between them and whoever might be looking for them.

Chapter 5

~

A few weeks later John got a call from Linda. She was planning Mike's retirement party and wanted to make sure John and Rhonda could come. Rhonda had gone grocery shopping. Mike asked Linda if he could call her back in an hour or two. After Rhonda returned home Mike phoned Linda back and told her they would be there. Linda gave him the address of the event venue. She promised the invitation would be mailed out in the next day or two and made John promise not to tell Mike about the party.

Thursday morning John and Rhonda drove to Mobile to catch a flight to Houston. After arriving in Houston, they picked up a rental car. The retirement party wasn't till Friday night. But John and Rhonda had decided to visit some old friends. When asked, they said they lived in a small town in Alabama. They didn't give many details beyond that. They mostly deflected the questions with some of their own. After visiting some of their old friends, they went to the hotel.

The next evening, they went to the address on the invitation. It was in an affluent part of town. John was glad Rhonda had talked him into wearing his coat and tie. Once inside, John recognized some of the faces from the CIA offices. He usually didn't do so well with names. Finally, Linda found them and hugged their necks. She pointed out a few friendly faces from their old church. John and Rhonda visited with them for a while. The trick they had learned was to visit just long enough to avoid too many questions about their new life in Alabama.

The retirement party was fun. They kept moving around and John introduced Rhonda to some of the people he had worked with in the CIA. Rhonda was particularly interested in meeting Luke Morgan. He had been very instrumental in helping keep the reporters at bay when they lived in Houston. That Prophet X program John had written had very nearly cost them their lives and had ultimately been the reason they were relocated to Alabama.

"Luke Morgan, this is my wife, Rhonda."

"Hello Luke, I know it's a little late, but thank you for helping us in Houston. You can't imagine how much that news interview you did helped us."

"Well, I can't really take the credit. The agency needed it and I was the one they picked to do it. I'm glad it helped. I'll have to tell you, this guy here had us all guessing for a while there."

"I know! He's a real knucklehead. He gets in more trouble. But he's my knucklehead and I guess were stuck with each other."

They all laughed politely. John scanned the room and saw McGuire. John excused them and they made their way over to McGuire.

"Rhonda, this is Bill McGuire. He's the one that signs the checks and gives the orders here in Houston."

"Well, don't believe everything they tell you. Rhonda, I'm so glad to finally meet you. I often wondered what kind of woman could keep this guy in check, for what 25 years now?"

"Nice to finally meet you too. And it ain't easy living with this hot mess, I'm tellin' you."

They all laughed. As McGuire was leaving them, he leaned in and whispered into John's ear. "We need to have a little chat. I'll have someone call you Monday."

John hated the wait. But he had no choice.

Sunday morning, they attended church with Mike, Linda, and the girls before the flight home. As they ate lunch Mike told John that they were planning on moving to Foley, Alabama. It was about 30 minutes from John and Rhonda's house. John was happy to hear his friend would be close. Finally, someone to talk to. Mike indicated they would be moving in a month or so. He promised to let John help when they were moving in.

The following Monday, McGuire's administrative assistant, Sue, phoned John to schedule a meeting with McGuire. They would meet in McGuire's office the following Wednesday. Sue said she would book the flight and asked if John needed a hotel room. That was a tricky one. John had no idea what the meeting was going to be about. John told her he didn't think he'd need the hotel room. So, she booked the return flight that same evening.

The next Wednesday John arrived back in Houston and was in McGuire's office for the 9AM meeting. Not a good sign, no one else in the room. John shook McGuire's hand and sat down as McGuire shut the door. McGuire congratulated John on the work he had done on the previous projects he had been on. John got the feeling he was being buttered up for something. He guessed McGuire would get to it eventually.

"John, how did you feel working as lead on your last two projects?"

"It was fine. I've been the lead on projects before."

"Yes, but these were not programming development projects. They were different than everything you did at the utility company, weren't they?"

"Yes, they were different." John guessed McGuire would come to the point sooner or later.

"Mike tells me you took to the project lead roll like a duck to water. But, just between you and me, I think he likes you a little too much."

"John, with Mike leaving, we are going to need someone to fill his position. I'm thinking you'd be about the best candidate at this point. You'd have to be full-time. No more of the contractor stuff, and you'd need to leave the utility job. We could let you stay in Gulf Shores for a year or so. But we'd want you somewhere here local and in the office four days a week."

"McGuire, to tell the truth, I'm really going to have some problems with the way we serve the American people. I've seen firsthand how the CIA can treat people who have things they want. I appreciate being pulled in and given a chance to change the methods we use from time-to-time. But I realize that there will be times when my best ideas are just not going to yield the same results as the old ways. I don't ever want to be the one to make that decision. For this reason alone, I don't think I'd be a good choice to fill Mike's position."

"John, we have dozens of experienced field operatives that have put in the time, earned their credits, and would love to have a shot at Mike's job? And here I am practically handing it to you on a silver platter. Let me be frank, Mike liked having you on his projects. He, and I, felt you brought something valuable to the table. With Mike gone, I'm not sure if the other teams will value your input the way Mike and I do."

"Mr. McGuire, I can't tell you how much I have enjoyed working with the CIA. I find it very interesting work. But as you pointed out, my lack of experience is another reason I don't think I would be a good fit for Mike's job."

McGuire looked across the table at John in silence. After an acceptably long pause, "John, this is a one-time offer. You're not likely to be in this position ever again. You do understand that, right?"

"Yes, I hate to disappoint you. But, I guess the bottom line is, while I enjoy helping the teams, I'm afraid, when it comes down to it, I'm really not cut out for this kind of work."

McGuire was disappointed. He wanted John for the job partly because he knew John didn't want the job. He knew John didn't crave the power as most all of the job applicants would. He knew John would always consider the job a burden.

"Well John, I had to try. I do understand your position and I hope we can still count on your help from time-to-time. You are valuable to this office."

"Absolutely. I'll do whatever I can to help out. Was there anything else?"

"No, I guess not. Suddenly I find that, thanks to you, I have a lot of interviews to start lining up. Thanks."

"McGuire, I have really enjoyed working with you and the teams. I really hope this will not change that in the future."

"Of course not. You're an asset we need. Thanks for coming in."

They shook hands and John left McGuire's office uncertain if his CIA days were over or what.

John had arranged to have lunch with Ricky Riley and the members of the NSA's AI Cryptography team. The discussion was a deep dive into the technical advances they had made after John's visit. They had a prototype of the new encryption scheme ready for roll out. It had passed through all the tests unscathed. She once again asked John if he'd like to be a part of the CIA's or the NSA's cryptography teams. They were currently sharing the work on their separate AI systems. John declined. At that moment, it occurred to John he had turned down two jobs, in the same day. It was these type coincidences that always got John to rethink his present course. He enjoyed the technical discussions even though some of the acronyms were lost on him.

After lunch John phoned Mike and asked his opinion about McGuire's offer.

Mike was reluctant to admit it, but in the end, he too felt the job was not a good fit for John.

"John it was always McGuire that suggested we bring you in on certain projects. My guess is he will still want you to come on board as a consultant on certain projects that he thinks will benefit from your input. Just don't expect all the team leaders to be as receptive as I was."

"Thanks Mike. I hate the thought of working without you. But in a way, I'm happy you're getting out of the slime bucket and going to live with us regular folks again."

They had a good laugh and then said their goodbyes.

It was time for John to make his way back to the all too familiar rental car return at Bush Intercontinental Airport. At least he'd be home with Rhonda and sleep in his own bed tonight.

Chapter 6

~

Friday morning John got up early and made some biscuits. He hadn't made biscuits from scratch in years. At one time, when the kids were little, he would make them every few weeks. He really liked cooking. And it was starting to show on his waistline. He had a pound of bacon laid out to go with the biscuits and some eggs.

Rhonda shuffled into the kitchen for a cup of coffee. "What's the occasion?"

"Well, I haven't made biscuits in a while and I wanted to see if I remembered how. Besides, I need my strength. I'm getting my hair cut this morning."

"Well, Sampson you aren't. But breakfast sure does sound good. So please do carry on and try not to make a huge mess in the kitchen, please. "

"Yes mam."

John was long overdue for a haircut. He pulled into the barbershop parking lot at 9:5 AM. They had just opened. Jim Dancer had been cutting John's hair since they moved to Gulf Shores. Jim knew most people around town as either clients or topics of conversation. John had learned to enjoy the unique challenge a barber's chair brought. For thirty minutes he was captive in that chair and the barber could ask him anything he wanted. How do you talk to someone about yourself without telling them anything about yourself, for thirty minutes, every two weeks, for almost two years, and not tell them a bunch of lies? Interesting problem. It was a challenge. John thought of it as something like chess. Steer the opponent into a conversational area you want and away from things you didn't want to talk about. It was just the sort of challenge John happened to like.

Jim said hello and motioned John over into the chair.

"Hello, Jim. Trim me up and make me look good. I got a hot date tonight."

"John, you want someone that works miracles you're going to have to go down the street to the Catholic church." They both laughed.

"John, do you have an Arabic looking friend that might be looking for you? Said he knew you from Houston. Hey, you never said you spent time in Houston. You ever been to Minute Maid Stadium?"

John suddenly had alarm bells going off in his head. Not in a full panic, yet.

"Jim did the guy give you a name?"

"Yep, he told me his name. Trouble is, I can't remember it. It'll come to me in a minute. I don't see many Arabic looking gents in this place."

"Yes, I went to Minute Maid Stadium once and watched a baseball game. I forget who was playing. I think a friend from Houston invited me."

Jim continued trimming John's hair and they chatted about baseball for the next ten minutes or so.

"His name was Hossein something another. The last name started with a 'K'. I don't think I quite caught it. Any way he said you might remember his brother that was a taxicab driver in Houston."

John only knew of one cab driver in Houston. It was the one he had killed after the guy had started shooting at them, about two years ago. It was difficult for John to focus on the rest of Jim's barber chair conversation. As he got up to pay Jim for the haircut he asked, "This Arabic looking guy, did you cut his hair?"

"No, Terry over at the hardware store sent him over here. He wanted to know where you lived, and she didn't know. When he asked me, I told him you had a place on the west side of town. But you never said exactly where it was."

John handed Jim a twenty-dollar bill for the haircut. "Thanks Jim, until next time."

As he was walking to his car John's brain was suddenly running through defensive moves again. The Hossein 'K', Arabic guy had to be related to that taxi driver named Jibril in some way. If he was, then he had managed to track John all the way to Gulf Shores. That could only mean this guy was very, very seriously focused on finding John for some reason. That reason likely had something to do with the taxi driver that John had shot. Whatever this guy's reason for looking for him was, it couldn't be good. How he had found John was another question. But that didn't matter at the moment. John had to get things moving if he wanted to get in front of this guy.

John phoned Rhonda from the parking lot. "Hello."

"Hey babe, it's me. I need you to do me a favor. Go upstairs and look up and down our street. Tell me if there are any new cars parked on our block."

The beach house layout had all the cars and laundry on the ground level with two levels of the main house above that. She would actually be on the third level, looking down on the street.

"Why?"

"You know me. Just playing a hunch."

"OK. I'm upstairs and looking out the guest room window. Nope, no new cars anywhere on the street."

"Thanks, I'll be home in ten minutes. I'll explain when I get there. Do me one more favor. Make sure the outside doors are all locked and don't answer the door."

"John, what's going on?"

"Look, it may be nothing. I'll fill you in when I get home."

John hung up and headed for the house. He was still deciding what he wanted to do. He checked his rearview mirror. No one seemed to be following. He randomly turned and went around a block just to see if anyone followed him. No, no one was following him.

When John got home, he used the secure line to call Mike. Mike could make some phone calls. But he was officially retired now and no longer had access to the Houston building or CIA computer systems. Next, John phoned McGuire.

"Hello John. Reconsidering my offer?"

For a brief second the scent of a CIA setup flashed in John's mind. But that didn't really track either. They likely had nothing to do with this.

"Sorry, no. I'm calling for another reason. I think we have someone looking for us. People in town tell me an Arabic guy named Hossein 'K' something has been asking around town for me. He mentioned he knows the taxi driver I shot. McGuire, I'm thinking someone has tracked us down and we need some support. At the very least, we need a little help getting this guy off us."

"Who told you this stuff?"

"It doesn't matter. What matters is that there is a guy hunting us."

"John, I'm sorry about this. Listen, get packed and plan on being gone for a few days to a week. I'll have a team out of the Mobile FBI office there in eight hours. They owe us a few favors down there. You guys just take a short vacation and I'll call you when it's over. They will get this guy and find out why he's looking for you. You guys should be back home in a week to ten days. It sounds like our priority is to see who he is first and then determine how he found you. Then, we can decide what to do from there."

"OK, sounds good. McGuire one more thing. I'll have to call you in a few days to see where we are on this. We're going dark for a few days. No cell phones and no tracks. Until this is behind us, we're not taking any chances of anyone tracking us."

"Understood. Good luck John. Be safe." And John hung up.

John told Rhonda and his daughter Amanda what was happening. That evening John took a walk. He left from the rear of the house and cut through the back neighbor's yard. Once on the street he walked to the Porter's house. He retrieved the envelope he had hidden and the Porter's car from the garage. He had removed a note from the envelope and placed it and a one-hundred-dollar bill on the work bench before closing the garage door. The note explained that he had borrowed their car and it would be left in the parking lot at the Mobile airport.

John drove to the street behind their house. Rhonda and Amanda came out through the backyard of their neighbor's house directly behind theirs. They each had two suitcases. John put the suitcases in the car's trunk. After placing their cellular phones in a Faraday bag, they left for the Mobile airport. A Faraday bag blocked all the signals to and from the cellular phones. This effectively blocked all tracking via their cell phones. It also prevented them from receiving or making any phone calls as long as the phones remained in the bag.

Before leaving the house, John had gotten Sue, at McGuire's office, to book their airline tickets and hotel reservations under the name Adison. Sometime back, Mike had gotten copies of their real driver license made with the last names changed to Adison. They had them made just for this type of situation.

They were going to Houston tonight and John had contact information for all of their Texas friends in the envelope. The plane ride from Mobile was uneventful. After picking up the rental car in Houston, they ate dinner and drove to the hotel.

The next morning, after breakfast, John phoned an old friend on the hotel lobby phone. He had met this guy at the church they attended until they were relocated. His friend's wife, Margie, answered the phone. John immediately recognized her voice. After a few minutes of catching up, John asked if he could speak with C.L., her husband. There was a moment of silence, then Margie told John that his friend had passed away the month before. John felt a sudden pain. He hadn't even known C.L. was sick. A lot can happen in two years. John asked if they could take Margie out to eat dinner. John was relieved when she said yes.

That evening they went out to eat. John and Rhonda resisted the urge to ask Margie about her husband's death. Instead, they focused on her and how she was doing. As John walked Margie back to her door, he hugged her and softly said "Sorry, I wasn't here for you." She was his sister just as if she had been a blood relative. He hurt for her loss. As she turned to go inside, they both caught the glistening of the moist eyes on each other's face. Nothing more needed to be said.

A white panel van pulled into the Davidson's driveway. The team from the Mobile FBI office went into the house. There were four of them. Jimmy Hudson was the electronics technician on this team. He walked around the front and back yards, discreetly placing small devices in tall grasses, bushes, and other places of concealment. These were very small, wireless, motion sensitive cameras. This was their parameter security screen. Next, he set up his laptop and the monitors to display what the outside cameras were seeing. The other agents made sure the house was empty and checked every exterior door and window to make sure everything was secure. All they could do now was wait.

The next morning, they had just finished shift change when a car pulled up on the curb across the street from the house. The driver just sat there and watched the house for a while. Too long a while. One agent slipped out the back door and positioned himself to get behind this guy if he walked up the Davidson's driveway. When he was in position, he had a good view of the car. He whispered over the radio, "Hey, guys the guy in the car looks Arabic to me." and then he read the license plate so a trace of the car could be started.

After about fifteen minutes the car door opened. The guy walked across Davidson's driveway. He paused briefly, pulled a Glock handgun from the small of his back, racked a round in the chamber and proceeded to walk up the short driveway. Things were happening fast now. Too fast to get the local police or sheriff's office in the loop.

They let the guy get on the front porch. When he rang the doorbell, the outside agent quickly approached him from the rear with his gun drawn.

"Hands up! Keep your hands where I can see them! Drop the gun! "Now slowly turn towards me."

After the suspect turned the front door opened where two agents were standing with guns drawn. They put handcuffs on the suspect. They packed him and everything they had brought back into the van before leaving.

He would be questioned and charged later. But not here at the Davidson house. They had local law enforcement tow the car to an impound lot after they had searched it.

Early Monday morning, John phoned McGuire to see how things were progressing. McGuire didn't want to discuss it on the phone and told John to come to his office at ten that morning. At that meeting McGuire told John, "We got your Hossein guy and that taxicab driver you shot a few years ago was his brother. He was coming for revenge, instead he's going to get some prison time and then he will be deported permanently."

John was taken back to that morning almost two years ago. The guy was shooting at the car Rhonda was in. Rhonda had just backed out of the garage and was still sitting in their driveway. John had grabbed the hunting rifle and ended the threat. It had all happened so fast. That's one of the reasons why they were relocated from Houston to Alabama.

"Thanks, McGuire. Just two questions. First are we cleared to go back home?"

"Yes. We haven't found anyone that was working with him. You and your family should be safe there."

"Secondly, how many brothers did that taxicab driver have?"

"Just the one that we know of. Our Israeli friends are checking the family out for us. Their investigation will be very thorough. But we do know he has a sister. We've already flagged her name with immigration. If she tries to come into the country, we'll know it."

John thanked McGuire and left the CIA building.

Chapter 7

~

Before heading back to Mobile, they had a nice dinner with Daniel, their son. He had lived in Houston for the past few years while they were in Gulf Shores. He had drifted from one minimum wage job to the next. With his income, roommates were a necessity that didn't tend to work for very long.

Amanda had spent the previous day and night with her brother. They had some news for John and Rhonda. They agreed to meet at a restaurant named Hofbrau Steaks, near the hotel. It was a weeknight, so there were plenty of empty tables and no waiting to be seated. At dinner Daniel and Amanda both announced they were both going to apply for college. Daniel wanted to stick with a college in Texas. Amanda wasn't sure where she wanted to go. They had a great dinner. They enjoyed being together. It seemed like such a long time since they were all together.

It was time to head back home, to Gulf Shores. They turned in the rental car and boarded the plane at Bush Intercontinental Airport. The flight was full. Someone got sick before the cabin door was closed and they were taken off the plane. After so many trips, John was really starting to hate the flight between Houston, Texas and Mobile, Alabama. But Amanda and Rhonda seemed to enjoy it.

The following week, John phoned Mike to see how retirement was treating him. Mike and Linda were packing and having a garage sale. They were set to close on a house in Foley the following week. John mentioned the great dinner they had with the kids and that they both were going to give college a try.

A few days later Mike phoned Daniel and asked him if he would be interested in a scholarship. Daniel said sure. Mike gave him a contact to call. Daniel ended up with a little-known scholarship that paid about half his tuition each semester at Texas A&M.

Amanda would be graduating from High School with honors later that year. Her college choices were a few months away yet.

When Daniel moved to the college campus, he realized just how few possessions he really had. All his clothes and everything else he owned fit in the backseat and trunk of his car. The dorm room was normal size, but it was designed for two people. Daniel started hauling his clothes into the dorm room. The small closet and drawers were filling up fast. His next stop was the registrar's office to pick up his class schedule. Then, he went to the campus bookstore. He could not believe the price of the books he needed.

John wouldn't be wondering what to do with the money he got for selling the government his program much longer. College was astronomically expensive. He realized the money had been provided at just the right time to meet their needs for the kid's college. God seemed to always know what they needed before they did.

Daniel soon met his roommate. His name was Jerry. He was a muscular guy who easily outweighed Daniel by fifty or more pounds. His large calves were only eclipsed by his huge arms and shoulders. Daniel soon learned this guy was from a small high school in Missouri. He was on a full scholarship for the weightlifting team. Apparently, he had won several national high school championships and gotten a scholarship. In contrast, Daniel was lean and had long slender muscles. While not nearly as big as his roommate, Daniel was much quicker and fluid in his movements.

The next week classes started. Daniel was focused on the new job. That's the way he thought about college, as a job. He was learning to get a degree, to get a better paying job, to live more comfortably. That was his current job.

After the first month at school, Daniel found a listing on a bulletin board. It was an advertisement for a security guard job. It was part time, at night and would let him study while making money. Perfect! He applied and soon was fitted for the mandatory security guard uniform. The job turned out to be just as advertised, He made rounds every hour. These took all of ten minutes. Then, he had 50 minutes to study.

A few weeks in, a guy dropped by the dorm room and introduced himself as president of some fraternity on campus and invited Daniel to a party the following Friday. Daniel happened to be off that Friday night and decided to stop by for a few free beers. While there, he met a bunch of immature kids, straight out of high school, drinking and partying. There were some girls there. Most of them were drinking and getting stupid. One of the girls he saw was sort of reserved considering all the partying going on. She wasn't the popular type of girl. She had that inner beauty that Daniel had grown to appreciate. She was beautiful inside and that showed outside. The fact that she was good looking didn't hurt. She was with the crowd, but seemed to stand apart from the others. She would hang back and watch the other girls. Daniel wanted to meet her.

He watched for an opening and soon found one. He introduced himself and asked her name.

"I'm Margo Campbell."

"Do you know any of the other people?"

"No. Not really. I was invited by a girl in our dorm."

"Same here. Do you like the party?"

"Not really. I just wanted to meet some people."

"Me too. Do you want to go someplace with a little less noise? Maybe get some coffee or something?"

"Sounds good. It's way too loud in here for me."

Daniel took her to a coffee bar and they talked for several hours before he took her to her dorm room. At her dorm room door, he wanted to kiss her. But he settled for her phone number instead.

A week later as he was leaving the campus to go shopping, his car wouldn't start. A few guys saw him under the hood of his car and asked if they could help. A few of the guys actually seemed to know a little about cars and quickly diagnosed the problem as a starter problem. They took Daniel to the local Auto Zone and he purchased a new starter. Two hours later the car started right up.

After a few months, John and Rhonda went to the Texas A&M campus to visit Daniel and see how he was getting along. Over dinner, he told them about his classes and a girl he had met named Margo. Everything seemed to be going well. They told him about Amanda's being accepted to the University of Arkansas for Medical Sciences. She wanted to be a nurse and would be attending school near enough to visit her grandparents often.

The following semester John and Rhonda were helping Amanda move to her dorm in Jonesboro, Arkansas. By the second semester Amanda had already started dating a guy from one of her classes. They both had too many classes to be seriously involved with anyone.

Chapter 8

~

After Amanda got settled in, John and Rhonda drove back to Gulf Shores. Their house felt strange with just the two of them in it. But they soon adapted to the change.

It seemed like things were once again starting to settle into a routine. John teleconferenced in on project meetings for the CIA a few times a week. The rest of the time he was dialed into the utility company's computers, building applications, and tweaking automated systems he had built for them. They were becoming regulars at the local church on Sundays.

One evening John was walking the neighborhood and he saw Ron Porter in his garage. "Hello Ron."

"Hi John. How's things going?"

"Smooth sailing this week. I never really thanked you for letting us borrow your car. It really means a lot to us to have friends like you guys. We could have been bank robbers for all you guys knew. If you have a minute I'd like to explain."

"Sure, I love a good story."

"I wish that's all it was. I want to tell you the back story about Rhonda and I. But, Randy you got to promise not to ever tell anyone. A lot of bad things can happen if people start figuring out who or where we are."

"Mums the word. I will not tell anyone your secrets. You want to pinky swear?"

They laughed. Then John told him about the Prophet X program, people coming to their house with guns, people chasing them all over Europe, how he had come to work for the CIA and finally about shooting the taxicab driver. Then he explained about the guy looking for them in Gulf Shores.

Ron had heard from another neighbor about the car getting towed from in front of John's house. So, he knew that part of John's story had to be true.

"So, that's y'all's big secret? What's your next big adventure going to be?"

John hadn't told him the part about the Switzerland angel encounter. He was always hesitant to tell others about that. It suddenly occurred to John that he hadn't discussed religion with Ron at all. He made a mental note to have that discussion with Ron sometime soon. But for today, John felt he needed to give Ron some time to consider everything he just learned about them.

"Man, we just want to be normal, like you and Rita, for the rest of our lives. It just seems to be taking us a long time to get past all that Prophet X stuff. I've kept you too long. I really didn't mean to bend your ear for so long. Besides, Rhonda will be wondering where I got off to. Randy, thanks for being a good friend and neighbor. See ya latter."

After dinner, John dialed into the utility company's network. He wanted to check on some modifications he had made to an automated process. He was having trouble with the connection. He rebooted their router and connected to the utility's network again. The same problem occurred again. Something was not connected as well as it was before. He tried unplugging and reconnecting all the ethernet cables. Perhaps someone had bumped into one of the cords and it was no longer plugged in all of the way. He noticed a screw was not tightened all the way on the wall plate of the ethernet connection into the wall. He got a screwdriver and started to tighten the screw, but then thought perhaps something in the junction box might be loose as well. So, he removed the wall plate. He just stared at the junction box for a minute. Then he replaced the junction box cover. There was a device attached to the cables. It was some sort of listening device that was powered by the ethernet. John checked the rest of the wall plates in the house and found two other similar devices. The next day he took the cars in to a small mechanic shop and asked them to change the oil and rotate the tires. He paid the young guy doing the work an extra twenty to hoist the cars up and let him look under them. They were hidden in the frame. But John found what could only be GPS trackers on each of the cars. Before he said anything to Rhonda, he needed to assess this new information.

After a few days John was pretty sure the tracking and listening devices were put in by the CIA. It probably happened around the time they had left so the FBI could be in the house to catch that cab driver's brother. John wanted to be smart about handling this. No need to rush it. He wanted to get his ducks in a row before he let the CIA know he knew about the devices. It was understandable that they might want to keep better tabs on him and what he was doing. He had looked for hidden video devices that might be in their home. But he didn't really know what to look for and found none. All his documentation was stored on a thumb drive. They probably had installed a key logger or some spyware on his desk computer. He had taken his laptop and the thumb drive with him. So, the laptop computer might still be safe to use.

That evening, during their walk around the block, John told Rhonda what he had discovered. They decided to just act normal for now. But they would only talk about the Porters when they were outside. John had hidden another envelope in the Porter's garage. The CIA hadn't asked him how they got to the airport in Mobile. That meant one of two things. Either they already knew about the Porters or they were too focused on catching that bad guy to follow-up on it. John thought the latter was most likely the case. At least he prayed it was.

John sat in the cool breeze, on the back porch, listening to the endless waves crashing on the beach. He needed a plan for dealing with the tracking and listening devices. It seemed that this was a good time to make a clean break from the CIA. Even though he didn't find them, he still had a nagging suspicion that there might be some video surveillance cameras hidden about the house. He wanted a clean break, another new beginning. Whatever they decided to do, they needed to divert the CIA from knowing about it until they did it. Sort of like jerking a band aid off. That would greatly limit the CIA's options and give him more control over the situation. He needed a way to leave all the surveillance devices behind them. It was starting to feel like they might need to move again. The beach sure was nice for the first few years. But now that the newness had worn off, it was not so great with the ever present sand and salt to deal with. While they washed the cars frequently and they didn't show it, he figured the salt had probably gotten a good bite on the cars after two years on the gulf coast beach. Maybe best to leave them and their tracking devices in Gulf Shores. The move, a new house, new cars, new cellular phones, a new desk computer. This was going to cut into their savings account. The Lord had always provided for them, and John figured this would be no different. He still had his utility company job. There were a lot of moving parts to keep up with. He'd need Rhonda's help.

John was wondering how he could use the tracking or listening devices to his advantage. It would be nice to at least dangle a carrot and see if someone would grab it. How to bait the trap? That was the question. What information would they, whoever they were, act on. John needed to talk to Mike. He didn't want the trap to backfire on him.

Mike and Linda had moved into their new place in Foley the week before. John hadn't wanted to bother them. But now he felt it was a good time. He had asked at the barber shop about gun stores in the area and had been given a few contacts. John drove to Mike's new address. It was 45 minutes from their house in Gulf Shores. Mike was flattening some moving boxes in the garage when John pulled up, unannounced in the driveway. Mike and Linda showed John their new home. After the greetings were over Mike and John sat on the back patio drinking some cold lemonade. "We're so glad to see you. But I suspect you've got something on your mind."

"I need some advice."

"You must really be in deep trouble to ask me for advice. You're the thinker not me. I just did what they told me."

"I found some tracking devices on our cars and listening devices in the house. I'm not sure that I found all the surveillance stuff. But I think it all got installed when that taxi driver's brother came looking for us. The CIA could have easily slipped in after the FBI left. I don't have any reason to suspect the FBI did it. Anyway, I think it's time for us and the CIA to go separate ways. I was wondering what advice you might have for me."

"John, I don't know anything about it. They wouldn't necessarily tell me anyway because I was on my way out to pasture. My guess is it is an internal department thing. McGuire might not know anything about it either. Did you remove the devices?"

"You know me better than that. I'm not touching them until I am sure they are of no use to me. I was thinking about dropping a bread crumb for whoever is listening."

"That could easily backfire on you."

"Yep. I'd need something juicy but not illegal; something that would start an investigation that leads nowhere. I document the fake intel in a letter to you. You hold on to it to prove my story. There will be an internal trail to whoever starts the investigation. What do you think?"

"John, that sounds like a very dangerous trap. The 'whoever' might have you eliminated as soon as they figure out you set a trap. McGuire might not be able to protect you. I would guess that this is another department, outside of operations. It's not McGuire's style to spy on his own people without good reason. I seriously doubt he has anything to do with the surveillance. Whoever it is, they're not likely to tell him about it either. Everyone knows he still likes you. God only knows why. You've always been such a royal pain."

"I'm thinking about screaming bloody murder about the surveillance devices a few days after I bait the trap. That will give them time to commit to an investigation or other actions before the devices are removed."

"John, John, John. Man, I'm glad you're a friend. You sure make one heck of an enemy."

"Mike, I'm thinking now would be a good time to enhance my personal protection. I asked around at the barber shop last week and found a few gun shops in the area. You want to come help me pick out some new guns?"

"Sure, I'm tired of moving boxes for the day. Do you want to go now?"

"Sounds good to me. But you had better check with the boss. Linda might have you scheduled for picture hanging this afternoon."

They were laughing and were soon out shopping for John's new pistols. He ended up buying two handguns and a rifle. He bought a Walther PDP PRO SD Compact 9MM with two extra magazines, a Kel Tec PMR30 22 magnum with two extra magazines, and a used Marlin 30-30. Mike actually purchased the guns and ammo. Later he would sell them to John after he fired them a few times each. This prevented a database check revealing that John had purchased these guns. It was not illegal to sell your personal guns to another individual, but it did prevent the government from knowing what guns you had.

Mike asked John why he wanted the 30-30 rifle. "Well, it's a short, sturdy gun. It can take some banging around and still take care of business. Its effective range is 200 yards. But at that distance you have to elevate above the target a fair bit. I hunted with one of these when I was about 12 years old. It's easy to carry and I just always liked shooting it."

Mike suddenly remembered John was an experienced hunter and an excellent marksman. But John would never admit it. The guns were purchased for protection, but the selected weapons were specifically for different types of hunting; hunting and eliminating threats. Mike remembered the other weapons John had. He remembered that John had a high-powered rifle, two shotguns, a 22 pistol, and several small 380 pocket guns. Not exactly an arsenal, but a nice variety of weapons for a variety of situations. Should trouble come for John or his family, it better not give John a chance to defend himself.

After a day at the gun range, Mike was feeling a little outclassed. He could shoot almost as good as John with the pistols. But John was raised using hunting rifles and shotguns. Mike just couldn't compete at the long ranges John was shooting the rifles.

John scheduled a lunch with McGuire the next week. At lunch John told McGuire that he suspected a security leak in the office. He didn't say whose office. When McGuire asked why he thought there was a leak, John said it was just a hunch. But he wanted to test it out to see if he was right. McGuire had learned to trust John's hunches. "What do you propose we do to test out your hunch?"

"First, I want to probe our communications. Easy way to do that without drawing attention is to drop a bread crumb and see if anyone picks it up."

"How would we do that exactly?"

"Easy, I'll call your office and report something that anyone listening will want to act on. You and I will know it's fake intel. But if someone else is listening then they might fall for it. It cost us nothing, its low impact, and if we have the right bait it will work. What do you think?"

McGuire thought about it for a minute. "OK, what do you think we should use as bait?"

"Well, I was sort of hoping you could help with that one."

McGuire thought about it for a minute. "Well, the best bait must be attractive to the type of fish we are fishing for. I can think of several lures: money, power, threat. But we don't know this fish and we don't know what he likes. We do know he is covertly spying on a consultant for my office. We know he likely has hooks into the FBI. Those were the guys staking out your house when we suppose the devices were installed. I think that's our lure. Tell me about a conspiracy between the FBI and CIA that you stumbled on. Tell me you found some evidence that someone in the CIA is conspiring with the FBI to defraud the public. Leave it vague, no details, no names, even if I ask. Tell me you placed all the documented evidence in a brown envelope, in the safe of that hotel you use when you're here at the Houston office. I'll take it from there. If we have the right bait, just maybe we will catch our fish."

"Sounds like a solid plan. When should I call you with this fake intel?"

"Give me two days to set the trap, then call me. Say Thursday afternoon."

"Sounds like a good plan. I'll call you Thursday around 2pm."

They finished their lunch and John headed back to the airport for the flight back to Mobile. On the flight home John was thinking Monday would be a good time for him to 'discover' the surveillance equipment at his house. John felt like David walking out to face a Goliath. Having McGuire in his corner helped.

Chapter 9

~

Thursday morning John phoned McGuire. "Hello, John. What's the occasion?"

"Hello Mr. McGuire. I have been trying to figure something out for a while and I'm just not making any headway. So, I thought I might need to just turn it over to you."

"That sounds pretty vague."

"Well, I stumbled across some coincidences in several of our past cases that seemed a little strange to me. I've been trying to connect the dots. But I just don't have enough information to put it all together."

"John, can you be a little more specific?"

"It looks like the FBI may be getting some information from the CIA on a regular basis. This information has nothing to do with the FBI as far as I can tell. There's not enough evidence to say for sure. But it sure looks like a leak in the CIA somewhere."

"John, do you have any proof of any of this or is this just speculation on your part?"

"A little of both at this point. The last time I was in Houston, I placed evidence of what I believe is a conspiracy in a brown envelope. That envelope is in a safe at the hotel I always stay at when I'm in Houston. At his point, it is just a bunch of coincidences. But it's suspicious. I was hoping you might look into it, as I'm at a dead end."

"John, we don't have the resources to squander on your hunches. I'll think about it. But you're going to have to convince me before I will be able to commit any resources to this."

"I understand. I'll keep looking into it and let you know if I find any concrete evidence."

"Was there anything else?"

"No sir. Thank you for taking my call."

John thought about how best to announce the discovery of tracking and listening devices the following Monday. A desperate call to McGuire, an outraged email to McGuire, his secretary, and all the team members he had worked with. Just to let everyone know he had been compromised, for how long he had no idea. McGuire would send a tech team to sweep the place and remove all surveillance equipment. They would also scan his computers for key loggers and spy ware. John had found one such rogue program on his desktop computer. He decided to leave it and see if the techs removed it or not.

At any rate, this would be a good excuse for John to part ways with the CIA. In truth he had been finding excuses to turn down more and more cases that they had asked him to lead. He hated the responsibility of being the project lead. He was a problem solver at heart and didn't like letting others do the heavy lifting. He relished doing the work, not reporting the work others did.

Tuesday, the day after his call to McGuire and his massive email, the techs showed up at his house. They located all the devices John had found and a few he hadn't. There were some pin hole cameras in the ceiling. He should have gone up in the attic and looked for them himself. He watched as they removed the trackers off his cars and one of the techs mentioned that they were not necessary as it was easy to hack someone's phone and track them using their phone. John found this most interesting. So, it was someone not up to speed on the tech stuff or someone who didn't have access to phone tracking data. Very Interesting.

The following Wednesday, after a cup of coffee, John phoned McGuire. "McGuire here."

"Mr. McGuire it's me John Davidson. I'm still not sure if we are not being listened to. But I wanted to tell you I think, considering the recent incident, that I might best be of service to some other department of the CIA."

"John, you're technically a contractor. You can't just move from one department in the CIA to another."

"I guess you got me there, Mr. McGuire. How do you propose we extricate ourselves from this situation?"

McGuire was backed into a corner. Not a place he was familiar with. "I guess we will just have to put you on ice for a while."

"On ice? What does that mean exactly?"

"It means we will not be calling you for a while."

"How long is a while?"

"A year or so at least."

"I see. Well, I would like to thank you for all the work you have sent my way. I have really enjoyed working with the CIA."

"Anything else?"

"No sir. Thank you."

After the phone was hung up. John felt lighter. A weight had been lifted. Time to move on.

The next week John and Rhonda started making plans to move back to Texas, near their old house. John was also looking at new vehicles in the Houston area. He decided the safe bet was to buy new phones and vehicles.

They had just gotten in touch with a realtor when John got a call from Arkansas. His dad was having some medical issues. John drove to Arkansas to be with his mom and dad. It was normally a long, eight-hour drive to his mom and dad's. He made it in seven hours. When he got there, the news was bad. His dad was already back home and on hospice. He was trending towards heart failure, due to the advanced stage of cancer, and was currently on morphine and Ativan. Over the next few days his dad was in and out of lucid states. Then, he was gone. The next few days after that were a blur. John knew it had happened. But the details illuded him. There were many family friends at the funeral. John only remembered seeing a few. The bond with his dad was strong and the loss was massive. It would be several days before John was fully functioning again.

After his father's funeral, it became apparent that their parents needed them back home in Arkansas. They decided to shift their destination from Houston to Arkansas. Being closer to home with family would be the best choice and one they gladly made. It would be nice to be back home where things were not as hurried and rushed.

John and Rhonda had dinner with Mike and Linda the following week. Mike greeted them at the front door. When they stepped into the house the aroma of fresh baked lasagna filled the house. It was one of Linda's favorite recipes. The dinner included a salad and garlic bread. For dessert they had strawberry cake.

During the dinner, John told Mike about how McGuire and he had handled the surveillance devices and how it had gotten him out of the CIA for the time being. He also told Mike about moving back to Arkansas. Mike and Linda hated to hear that they were moving. John and Rhonda promised to come visit them from time to time.

Mike asked John," Where in Arkansas are you planning on moving to?"

"We're not sure. We're still looking. But we decided to look for something outside of the city. Maybe south of Little Rock. Our families would only be about thirty minutes apart. That's the main reason we decided on Arkansas. With my dad being gone, I need to be closer to my mom. She can still take care of most stuff. But Rhonda's parents are about the same age as my mom, and they will need us more in the years to come. So, it just seems to be a good time to go home."

"Sounds like a good move."

"I checked the housing market, and we should make a good profit off the beach house sale. I checked on those papers we signed when we purchased the beach house from the government. Because it was a government auction and a greatly reduced starting bid, we were obligated to stay there for forty-eight months after the purchase. The forty-eight months ended last month. Then, there are the surveillance devices and that guy looking for us. Mike, I'm pretty certain all of this is God telling us it's time for a change. I just hope we're moving where He would have us move."

"You really see God in this?"

"Absolutely. He will confirm it when we move. You wait and see."

"How will He do that."

"I don't know. But He always shows me the path and gives me a peace about it. I just have to ask for and seek His guidance."

"John, I never thought of you like that. All I and everyone else can see is a smart guy making some pretty smart moves at the right times."

"Mike, I'm dumber than dumb on my own. All that stuff with the Prophet X program, the running, the evading, the way it all turned out. I couldn't do any of that stuff on my own. OK, I might have tried to do some of those things. But they would have failed a million ways if not for God's help."

"I don't think that there is anyone who has ever met you, that would agree with that."

Mike told John about the interdepartmental fighting at the CIA. Everyone wanted to discredit the other departments, so their own department could get a bigger cut of the budget. Then there were the power struggles and the back biting that goes on. Everyone was trying to use someone to get a foot up the food chain. John had never been anything but a contractor. So, he was never exposed to all the intra-office goings on. The more Mike told him, the more thankful he was that he didn't work full time for the CIA.

Chapter 10

~

John discovered that the five-acre lot was more than his mother thought she could handle alone. She wanted a smaller place, in town, closer to medical care and stores. Every week He and his younger brother, Bobby, took turns mowing the five acres with the John Deer tractor and grooming blade. It wasn't difficult work but something that had to be done.

John's mother put the house that she and his dad had built up for sale and started looking for houses in town. It only took a few months, and the house was sold, and she was purchasing a new house in Benton, Arkansas. She had a garage sale and sold everything she didn't want to move.

Over the next few months, John and Rhonda finalized the sale of their beach house in Gulf Shores. They purchased a house on a one-acre lot, just south of Little Rock, in an area called East End. Things were happening fast. His mother had moved, and now they too were moving. His brother had lived in Benton for the previous ten years. They would all be able to enjoy helping each other, playing games, and Sunday dinners. It would be much like old times, before John and Rhonda moved to Texas. Things were shaping up to be a time for making some sweet memories.

The week before their move from Gulf Shores, John sold their vehicles and purchased some new ones from a dealer in Foley. Rhonda purchased a van with all the newest gadgets and features. John purchased a new Jeep Rubicon. Jeeps were popular in Arkansas due to the occasional snow and ice conditions each winter. It wasn't deep snow, as only six to nine inches were typical, and it didn't stay long, a week or two at most. The black ice, however, caused a lot of people to end up in the ditches every year.

John and Rhonda found that they loved the rural life in East End. The H.O.A. (Home Owner's Association) back in Houston had made for some bad neighbors. Here neighbors actually talked to each other and tried to help each other. In Houston people just reported things they didn't like to the H.O.A.. In Houston everyone seemed separated. Here in East End, Arkansas everyone was a neighbor and they all helped each other. Things were more deliberate here. In Houston the tendency was to go out to eat every night. Here the tendency was to eat out of a well-stocked pantry. This was perfect for John and Rhonda. They both loved cooking together. They planned their meals for the week and bought groceries accordingly. In Houston they decided each night about suppertime what they would be eating; not a lot of thought or planning went into most meals. Everything was about 10 minutes from the house in Houston. Here it was a thirty-minute drive into town. Everything was planned, slower, more deliberate, and they preferred it that way.

There was a lot of work to do on their new home. The yard, in particular, needed some immediate attention. With no trees, they would need a riding mower. So, John started shopping for a zero-turn mower. He soon found one at Lowes and had it delivered to the house. He also had a storage shed delivered. Nothing fancy. Just large enough for the riding mower and yard tools. Over the course of the next month there was fencing in the back half-acre, sod, landscaping, planting flower beds and trees. Inside they had new appliances delivered and installed.

There was a grassy field behind their house. Sometimes, while sitting on the back porch, they would see deer feeding in the field. Then there were the squirrels always trying to steal some birdseed out of the bird feeders. It was nice to sit on the back porch, in the evenings, and watch the birds and animals in the field and trees behind their house.

Rhonda had gotten their internet hooked-up and was still working corporate travel from home. John was still working remotely for the utility company. Other than a new location and new cars, not much had changed. John was finding it much easier to say no on the rare occasion that the CIA asked him to do stuff. As a contractor, he could do that, up to a point without any consequences. But he suspected his default answer was going to be 'no' from here on out. Eventually they would stop calling.

Six months after the move to Arkansas, John planned a trip back to Houston. There were some old friends he needed to visit. While there he had lunch with his utility company boss, Don McCarthy. He and Don had been friends for a long time. Don was his boss. But Don had a unique outlook on employees under him. His philosophy was simple: 'get good people under you, that know how to do their jobs and stay out of their way' and that's what he did. John and Don met at Saltgrass restaurant in The Woodlands, Texas.

"Wow, it's been a while." John offered as he shook Don's hand.

"Yes, and you're quite the exceptional employee." Don responded.

They ordered and then Don asked about John's adventures. John gave him a brief re-cap of all that had happened and where he currently was. Don was astonished at the adventures his employee had encountered. Don told John that the work environment at the utility company was changing. The company was more focused on representing liberal ideals than actually getting cutting edge work from its employees. John was saddened to hear this. The utility company had always been focused on doing the best job it could until now. Now it seemed they were focused mostly on minority causes to champion and no longer concerned with attracting those with good work skills or moral ethics. The efforts of the utility company were now focused on outsourcing the real work and codifying minority groups internally. It appeared that proven talent and skills were no longer valuable assets to the company.

Don and John enjoyed the rest of their lunch talking about their families. Don shared that he was considering retirement. John was wondering where the next year would lead them. It appeared that everything was shifting and moving. Nothing was certain in these times of change. John thought about the old children's Bible story about a man that built his house on sand. Things were definitely shifting and changing. But John's house was built on a solid rock, his faith. Just because he didn't know where things were going to settle, didn't mean they were out of control. He knew God had a plan, even if he didn't see it.

The week John returned to Arkansas, it snowed. That was something Rhonda and he had not seen in many years. The ground was wet, and it had been below freezing the previous day. The snow accumulated over the next day and a half. John decided to try his hand at something he remembered from his childhood, snow ice cream. He put a ceramic mixing bowl in the freezer with a cup of heavy whipping cream and some vanilla extract. After it had chilled for forty-five minutes, he took the bowl outside and scooped some of the freshly fallen snow into the bowl. He mixed it with the heavy cream and vanilla. When he got inside, he added some sugar to the mixture. It turned out to be very good.

Chapter 11

The next several months were uneventful. John continued his work at the utility company. On the rare occasion he needed to attend a safety meeting of some sort, he would use the conference room at the local utility office. One thing that had always remained constant at the utility company was their required computer-based training classes. John could almost always take these on-line training courses from the comfort of his home. But occasionally, he would have to participate in a video conference and that meant being at an office somewhere. These were the touchy-feely programs that had absolutely nothing to do with the work the utility company did. It was only twenty minutes to the nearest office and these conferences were normally only a once-a-year deal.

John had been thinking about all the documentation he had. He had all of it stored electronically on a memory stick. The files were all encrypted with his special encryption program. But, given enough time an AI encryption program could break his encryption.

The next morning John took a drive to the local grocery store. He walked down the street to the pharmacy and asked to borrow their phone. He phoned his cousin, Randy Lamar. Randy had recently retired from a long career in designing and building specialized electronic equipment.

"Hello."

"Randy, this is John. How's it going?"

"OK, I guess. Did you get a new phone?"

"No, I just borrowed this one. I need a huge favor. I need a specialized electronic device built and I don't want anyone to know about it."

"What type of device?"

"I want a solid-state storage device that has hidden storage capabilities."

"You can do that with software."

"Yes, and a thorough storage media inspection will show it. I need a device that looks and feels like a small solid-stated drive, one terabyte should do, and has a hidden switch to access a separate memory stick hidden in the case. Does that sound like something you could build for me?"

"Sounds pretty simple. When do you need it?"

"The sooner the better. But don't do it if you have other projects going on."

"I need something to keep my mind sharp anyway. Maybe three weeks?"

"Sounds great, I'll plan to come visit you in four weeks. If you have any questions, give me a call and I'll go borrow another phone to call you back."

"Are you in trouble?"

"Nope, just planning for a rainy day. Thanks, I gotta run."

By that night Randy had most of the components figured out. He ordered a five-terabyte solid-state drive, a 32 gigabyte memory stick, a super small micro controller board, dual color micro LED, and the smallest eight-pin dip switch he could find. It would take a week or two for all the components to come in. Once he got the components, he would systematically remove all protective cases, and unneeded components to strip them down to be as compact as possible. But he had the sizes and specifications for all the components and could start on a prototype for the case. He had a new toy. It was a 3D printer. It would be perfect for making the case. He sketched out the device on a scratch pad and went to work with the 3D rendering software.

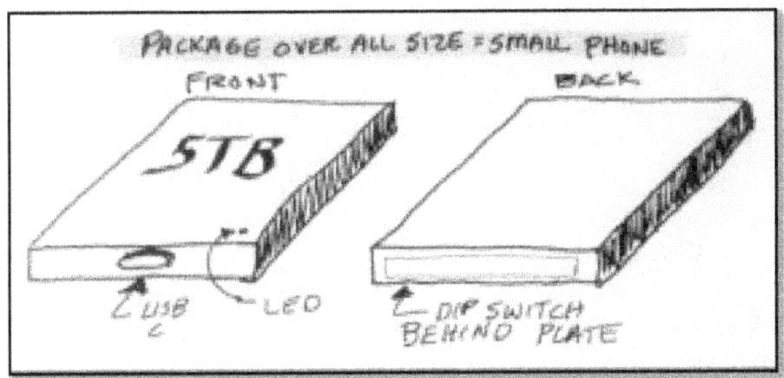

After he received all the components, he tested them for thermal variances under load. If there were going to be any hot spots in this device, it was best to identify them now and plan to dissipate the heat. Luckly with such small voltages and super-efficient components, the thermal test showed no need for heat shunting.

The next summer, the local news was full of violence in many big cities. Protests, gangs, and violence were destroying the businesses. There were reports of people in some cities being attacked at gunpoint for no reason at all. It seemed like the world was losing its mind. Local law enforcement was almost powerless to stop such widespread chaos. Stores were being looted and burned. But that was in the city, a place most of the people in the rural areas avoided when possible.

The small community near John and Rhonda's house was quiet. Most of the people had moved to this place to avoid the city, the taxes, and the city restrictions. Generally, people respected your privacy and only made inquiries because they were genuinely interested in seeing if they might help you in some way.

It was quite a shock when their small community heard rumors that the violence in town was moving to the surrounding rural areas.

A week later their small community was startled to learn that the one and only local grocery store had been vandalized. All of the windows were broken, many of the food products had been trashed, and there was some spray-painted graffiti on the floors and registers.

After dinner John and Rhonda discussed the situation while cleaning the dishes. John told Rhonda, "I think we need to be prepared, in case this thing escalates."

"Prepared, how?"

"I'm going to move the guns and ammo out of the closet. I want to put the guns where they will be handy. They will be loaded and ready for action. All you'll have to do is work the safety and pull the trigger."

"That sounds reasonable. But I'm not planning on doing the shooting. That's your job, not mine."

"I know. But you need to be able to take care of it, should a situation arise while I'm not here. I think I want to talk to the neighbors around us. I want to make sure we all keep an eye out for each other and have each other's phone numbers."

"Do you really think they will do anything on our street?"

"No, I just think having everyone's phone number is a good idea."

She knew John and how he thought through things. He was preparing for something, even if he didn't know what it was.

John loaded and staged guns near the doors and in each room of their new home. If something unexpected happened, he wanted to be ready. He took Rhonda to each of the guns and made sure she knew how to fire and reload the weapons.

John and Rhonda's new home was located on a dead-end street. That tended to limit the traffic. After some thought, John went to his neighbors and discussed the situation. He wanted everyone around them to be aware and watchful. He was preparing for the worst and praying for the best outcome. He made sure he and the neighbors had each other's cell phone numbers and were aware of the situation. John and Rhonda lived in the fifth house on the left-hand side of their street.

The street came to a dead-end a few dozen houses past their place. They knew most of the cars that belonged in the neighborhood. The two odd cars traveling together were noticeable. They drove slowly down and then back up the street. John had noticed the cars, and he was alarmed.

The neighbors across the street, Bryan and Melanie Henderson, were younger. Bryan had retired from the army as an Airborne Ranger. He was accustomed to tactical plans and helped John develop a few contingencies to protect their street. Neither of them thought the plans would actually be needed. They both saw the wisdom in at least discussing possibilities and strategies. Their discussion was about general ideas, tactics, nothing in the way of a firm plan. They both instinctively knew that should a situation arise; it would be too fluid to fit neatly into a preconceived plan.

They couldn't have known, but just two days later, their discussion would pay off. It was about six in the evening. Most of the people on their street were home, preparing dinner. The same two cars stopped in front of the Winston's home. The Winston's were an older couple. John had spoken to Mr. Winston about the rumors and discovered that he had a colt 45 that he hadn't fired in many years.

John phoned the Winstons and advised them of the situation unfolding in front of their house. Their house sat closer to the street than most of the other houses. This undoubtedly made them a prime target.

"Mr. Winston this is John Davidson. I see that there are some suspicious cars on the street in front of your house. Are you expecting company?"

"No. I don't know those kids. What do you think they want?"

"Nothing good. Could you and Mrs. Winston do me a favor? Make sure your front door is locked, go to the rear of your house, into a back bedroom, and get that 45 you said you have ready to defend yourselves. I'll call you later when they are gone."

"OK. What are you going to do?"

"Depends on what they do. Keep your phone near and stay in the rear of the house. We've got this."

"OK, our doors are all locked. Be careful."

Rhonda overheard John's phone call. "What's the matter?"

"Trouble. Go to the bedroom. Get the 12-gauge shotgun from behind the bedroom door. It's loaded. Do you remember how to work the safety?"

Rhonda immediately knew that John was focused on an immanent threat. He only gave commands and short answers when he was focused on a problem that needed an immediate solution. She knew that whatever the problem was, he had probably thought it through. That was John, always thinking, planning, and praying.

"Yes."

"Stay in the bedroom. I'll call when it's over."

She wanted more information. But now was not the time to play fifty questions. She did as he said.

John quickly gathered a few of the guns and ammunition that he had placed in various rooms of the house. He turned his attention back to the blinds in the front window.

Next, John phoned the Bagley's. They had two small children. Mr. Bagley had a 30-06 hunting rifle. John asked him to do the same as the Winston's. Mr. Bagley was a veteran and told John he would take a position at their front window.

John posted on the neighborhood Facebook page that everyone should stay in their homes until the bad guys were gone.

Lastly, John phoned Bryan Henderson across the street. Bryan and John quickly developed a plan. It was important to know where everyone was if guns were to be used. They each put their phones on vibrate. Bryan would take a position in the ditch by his driveway with his 308 rifle and a 9mm handgun. John would try to take up a position behind the rose bush planter in his front yard, near the street. Bryan phoned John when he got in position. John had taken his 243 high-powered rifle and the Kel Tec PMR30 as he got in position behind the planter. Both had made it to their vantage points unnoticed by the bad guys in the cars.

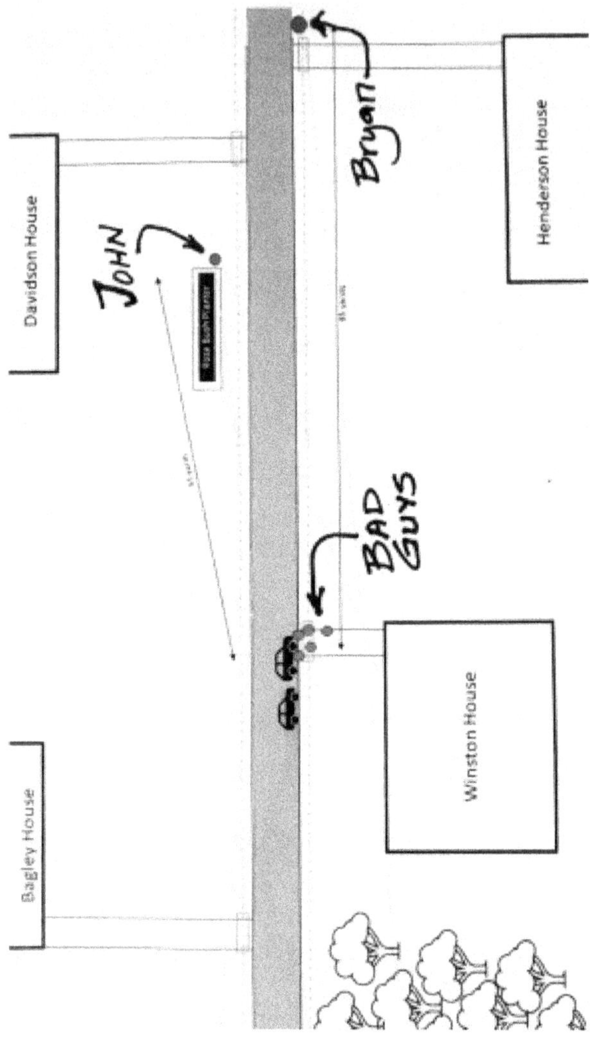

Davidson House
Bagley House
Henderson House
Winston House
John
Bryan
BAD GUYS

John would be shooting at a distance of sixty-five yards. He could easily pick a buttonhole at that distance if the buttonhole was stationary. These buttonholes would be practically dancing while they were shooting off their mouths and guns. John would need to aim for the center of their chest and pray his aim was true. Things would happen very fast once they started. He turned the gun's scope down to its lowest magnification setting. The problem was that at such a short distance he would need to use the iron sights instead. The scope mount was such that you could look under the scope and still use the iron sights. When things started happening, there wouldn't be time to search for targets in the scope. The planter was constructed using two rows of cinder blocks with two cinder blocks closing off each end. It was two cinder blocks tall and full of dirt. John could easily watch the bad guys from between the plants and not be seen. Perfect cover and concealment for the situation.

Bryan laid flat in the dry ditch, near the driveway culvert. He used the edge of the driveway as his cover and brace. Bryan would be shooting at about 85 yards, easily in his range. The 308 hadn't been fired in a while. Like John, Bryan took great care not to bump the scope or sights when handling his rifles.

The bad guys were getting out of their cars, and they all had guns. This could go south quickly. John phoned Bryan on his cell phone. After making sure Bryan was set, John told Bryan that he was going to take out one of the car's radiators as soon as the first shot was fired. They didn't have to wait long. One of the hoodlums fired a shot in the air to announce their arrival at the Winstons house to the neighborhood. A split-second later John fired the 243 at the center of the radiator of the closest car. The supersonic round made a crack and then a huge boom as the bullet broke the sound barrier. This literally rattled the windows in the nearby houses. Two of the five guys fell to the ground, shocked by the noise. They got up and assumed the shot had come from the Winston's house. At that point they all started firing at the Winston's house. John couldn't believe how bad things had suddenly gone. He had intended to scare the bad guys away. He couldn't let them kill the Winston's. John lined-up for a second shot. There were two of the bad guys standing lined up. John fired and they both fell. The others heard the loud gunfire and then they saw their buddies fall. Obviously, someone had just shot two of them. But the remaining three guys, not knowing where the shot came from, just kept shooting at the Winston house. A few seconds later, John heard the sharp sound of Bryan's 308 from his driveway. Another bad guy fell in the Winston's driveway. The other two finally got the idea that they were not going to win this battle if they stayed in the driveway. As they turned, they noticed the fluid pooling under the first car, and both jumped into the second car. As they started driving, having no other clear targets, they were shooting blindly out of the car windows. As they accelerated around the lead car John stood with the KelTec pistol gripped tightly with both hands and pointed as the car accelerated down the street towards him. He focused on the front and rear side windows of the four-door sedan. The guy in the back seat was firing in his direction. John started emptying the thirty-round magazine into the car's windows. At some point he felt more than heard the concussion of the 308 fire again. The guy in the rear seat disappeared and the driver had slumped over as the car idled over into the ditch. Both the occupants were dead.

The get-away car had traveled just 75 feet before coming to rest in the ditch. John ran around and approached the car from the rear. He peaked in the back seat to see an obviously dead bad guy. The front seat revealed the same. These guys weren't going to be causing anyone trouble anymore. Their guns were on the floor in a growing pool of blood. John could still hear the ringing in his ears from all of the shooting. He looked around and saw Bryan still prone in the ditch. Bryan gave him a thumbs up but stayed in place. He had his rifle trained on the Winston's driveway while John approached keeping the disabled car between himself and the three bodies on the driveway. When John looked around the car, what he saw on the driveway left no doubt. These guys would never bother anyone again.

After checking on the Winstons and Bryan, John phoned the Sheriff's department. It would take a while for them to arrive. Other than some bullet holes in the Winston's house, no one except the hoodlums and their car got shot. While waiting, John phoned McGuire and told him what had happened. McGuire asked John what county they lived in and said he would have someone contact the local Sheriff's department. Bryan and John put their weapons in their houses and sat on the rose bush planter, waiting for the sheriff's department to send someone. Not counting the casings that were likely lost in the grass, John and Bryan counted 36 bullet casings on the driveway. There were plenty of bullet casings scattered all over the driveway to see that these guys were shooting. There were more bullet casings in the car.

When John went inside Rhonda asked, "Is everything OK?"

"Not really. The bad guys all got shot."

"Anyone else hurt?"

"No, everyone is a little shaken up but otherwise fine."

"It sounded like a war out there."

"The bad guys started it, and we ended it. We were prepared, they were not."

"Do they need any medical assistance?"

John didn't say anything. It was the way he shook his head. She knew they must all be dead.

When Sheriff Johnson arrived, he snapped pictures and took notes as he interviewed everyone. At some point he called for the coroner and a wrecker for the cars. A little later another Sheriff car arrived. They talked for a few minutes and the unidentified officer left. Officer Johnson didn't confiscate any of their guns. Apparently, for some reason, the local Sheriff's department suddenly realized that people living in rural areas needed to be able to protect themselves.

Bryan had shot twice, one bad guy in the Winston's driveway and the get-away car driver. John had shot the radiator, two bad guys in the driveway and the bad guy in the back seat. He had fired the Remmington 243 twice and had emptied fifteen of the KelTec's thirty round magazine. Of the fifteen rounds John had fired at the moving car's windows, three had been stopped by the car door, just below the window. The rest had found their intended targets.

As the coroner performed autopsies on the five bad guys, he was able to establish that the guy in the back seat was shot 5 times and the driver was shot 6 times with the small but devastating 22 magnum rounds. The coroner found it impossible to definitively ascertain if the 308 or one of the 22 magnum rounds had ended the driver's life. But it was unlikely that anyone would ever care to challenge the report either way.

The Winstons couldn't thank Bryan and John enough for everything they had done. John kept trying to think of a way he could have better handled the situation. Once again, the thought that he had ended someone's life made him sick to his stomach. He couldn't stop thinking that there should have been a better way to handle the situation. But those guys seemed pretty determined to kill someone.

The following week, McGuire asked if he could come visit with John. John knew there was a reason for McGuire's visit. They arranged for dinner at John's house the following Tuesday night.

When McGuire arrived, John and Rhonda welcomed him in. They had dinner almost done. The dinner menu was grilled steaks, baked potatoes, and a salad. After dinner McGuire joined John on the back porch while John cleaned the grill.

"Well, I guess you'll tell me sooner or later. Did we catch anyone in our little trap?"

To John's surprise, McGuire said, "Yes, we're still investigating to assess the damage to the department. We haven't gotten very far yet."

"Who are they and why did they have our house bugged?"

"Not sure how or why that happened yet. Like I said, we're just getting started on the investigation. I was hoping you might want to help us look into it. I know I'd be pretty interested in getting some answers if someone put me under surveillance."

John was thinking about who exactly placed the surveillance equipment in their Gulf Shores house. Did McGuire already know? McGuire had just thrown out the bare hook. No bait to entice John back to working for them. Perhaps in his own way, McGuire was trying to make it easy for John to say no.

"Mr. McGuire, I appreciate the offer, I really do. But to tell you the truth, we've had to move twice and well, Rhonda and I would like to sit this one out.

"John, about this shooting. I understand it took place just a few houses down the street here."

"Yes. I took a position behind that cinder block planter out by the street. I figured it would stop anything they were shooting."

"Did it ever occur to you that they might have had the wrong address?"

"No. There were reports of vandalism in the city and even out here, at our local grocery store before this happened. Some of the people at church were talking about a home invasion and vandalism in a neighborhood not too far from us. That sort of stuff just doesn't happen out here in small communities. I think the bad guys just figured they could get away with some stuff since we don't have police out here."

"I see. Sounds like it may have just been a bad choice on their part. The report I read said you and a neighbor ambushed five bad guys."

"They pulled up and started shooting. Then I shot out the radiator to scare them away. But they just started firing on the Winston's house.

I had to do something before they walked up to the Winston's front door. They didn't know where the shots came from until it was too late."

"Did you really kill two guys with one bullet?"

"Relatively short distance and soft tissue. That caliber of bullet does some traveling before it stops. And I got lucky. The bullet never struck a bone in the first guy and just passed right through him. The second guy caught the bullet after it left his buddy. Just a lucky shot."

"You seem to be pretty good at making lucky shots. How long had you been planning for that scenario?"

"No planning for any specific situation. Given the events in Little Rock, it just seemed reasonable to talk to my neighbors and see where we were with guns and capabilities. I wanted to have that information ahead of time if trouble came down our street. You know, 'who had a gun?', 'did they know how to shoot?', 'how to call them should trouble happen'. Just basic stuff to better communicate and handle any problems. I had assumed that if we did have any trouble on our street that it would happen closer to the main road."

"Why did you shoot the radiator?"

"I figured they would be able to leave the neighborhood. But the car wouldn't make it very far, it would overheat, and the sheriff might catch them before they made it back into the city. That didn't work at all. The last two guys finally figured out they were going to die if they stayed there in the driveway. They saw the radiator fluid all over the ground under the first car. So, they jumped into the second car. Where they messed up is that they started firing as they drove towards us. Even if they made it past us, they were going to have to turn around and come back because this is a dead-end street. We basically had them in a gauntlet. There was no way they were leaving this street while they kept shooting. And they were shooting from the car. So, we stopped them."

"The Sheriff's notes indicated that you took one of your tennis shoes off after taking up a position behind the planter. What was that all about?"

"I guess I was a little rattled after the shooting. I shouldn't have mentioned that to the sheriff. I'd like to say it's an Arkansas thing, but it's not. The cinder blocks make for a pretty rough surface to brace the gun for a shot. I didn't want to scratch up the finish on my rifle. Besides it makes for a steadier shot when you have a rest that cradles the gun a little. Have you ever shot rifles much?"

"No. I'm a desk jockey these days. Never had much practice with long range shooting. We mostly focus on short-range handgun drills. As I recall, you once told us you didn't have much practice with moving targets. But the car was moving. Did you just get lucky again?"

"I've tried to expand my skills set somewhat since we did that interview. You'd be surprised what I've picked up from you CIA types."

"I'd say you've mastered the moving target now."

"Or maybe I was just lucky. Take your pick. With fifteen rounds fired, I was bound to hit something. It worked out anyway. It's probably a miracle they didn't shoot me before I shot them."

"Are you sure you don't want to come back and help us out on a few cases from time to time? You could really help us make a difference."

"Thank you. But considering everything that's happened, I think we had better not. Rhonda and I really just want a simple life for a while."

McGuire knew John had already made his decision and there wasn't much point in pushing the issue. John told McGuire how living in rural Arkansas differed from living just north of Houston. McGuire couldn't see the attraction. He preferred the nice restaurants and the city life in general. McGuire said his goodbyes early in the evening and left for a hotel in Little Rock. The next morning, he would be on a flight back to Houston.

Chapter 12

~

It had been about three weeks since John had talked to his cousin, Randy Lamar. He went to the pharmacy and borrowed their phone again to make a call. Randy had finished the memory device and John told him he would fly out to visit them in two days. The long flight took all day but was otherwise uneventful. They ate a great dinner at the Montana Club, in Butte and then drove to Sheridan. After arriving home, Randy took John into his project room. One wall was covered, floor-to-ceiling, with shelves packed with various pieces of electronic equipment and small bins of electronic components. John was immediately impressed with just how little he knew about electronics and electronic gear. The opposite wall didn't look so alien to John. It also had floor-to-ceiling shelving. John was familiar with these items. There were hand tools, sanders, drills, epoxy, glues, tape, fiberglass, various types of cordage, screws, nuts, bolts, sanders, typical hobby and craft supplies (he had a similar, but much smaller shelf at his house). On the far wall contained a work bench, a 3D printer, and a laser engraver/cutting tool. Tucked away under the tables were other assorted pieces of equipment. John recognized most of them. The vacuum pot and air compressor were the larger items under there.

Randy pulled open a drawer on the work bench. He retrieved a very polished and professional looking external, solid-state drive from his desk drawer. He turned to face John and took a small paper clip and pressed it into a tiny hole near the back of the device. As he did this, he slid a small portion of the rear of the device open. Under the hidden door was an eight-pin dipswitch. Randy slid the small door closed and it snapped into place. He handed the device to John. It looked and felt just like a factory-made solid-state drive. It was black with some glitter powder just under a high gloss finish. It was like holding a chunk of highly polished black glass. It was a work of art. Randy explained that the dip switches had to be set to a specific pattern to access the hidden memory stick. If the dip switches were set to any other configuration, then the device would read and write from the solid-state drive. If the switch was up, it was on, if the switch was down, then it was off. The number one switch had a red dot next to it. The switches represented a binary numbering system. Their values were 1, 2, 4, 8, 16, 32, 64, and 128. By setting all the switches off and turning the first, fifth and seventh up/on, the micro controller would read 81 from the dip switches and all reads and writes will be to a 32-gigabyte memory chip in the device. Set the dip switches to any other configuration and it will read and write to the five-terabyte solid-state drive. The small LED light would flash when reading from or writing to the device. If the solid-state drive was being accessed the LED light was red. If the memory chip was accessed, then the LED light would be green.

As John held the device and inspected it, he was astonished at the precision in the way the seams fitted together. You could barely make out the seams at all. Unless you knew it was there, the cover for the dip switches blended in with the base so well, you'd never notice it. The seams had been hidden in a small groove. After playing with the memory device for a few minutes, John asked Randy, "How much do I owe you?"

"Nothing. It was a fun project. It gave me an excuse to play with my new 3D printer. You got any other device builds in mind?"

"No, this one is all I think I'll need. Are you sure I can't repay you? The drive and memory chip had to cost something."

"Don't worry about it."

John flew home the next day. During the flight John pulled the Memory device from his pocket to look at it. The laser etching made this thing look very professional. There was some very small lettering etched along one of the edges. It was so small that john had not noticed it before. He had to hold the device at just the right angle to make out the micro lettering. It appeared to be a jumble of letters and some numbers.

NAP SOV PE'BE'LU'PU'BOGH RURNIS 101429.67

It would be several months later when John asked one of his friends from the encryption team at the CIA to run the cryptic message through their AI server to see if it could decipher the message. John laughed at the response. It was a pure Star Trek nerd thing and Randy Lamar loved Star Trek. The letters were a message in Klingon that read "WISDOM UNLOCKS THE KNOWLEDGE" and the numbers were the Star date equivalent of OCTOBER 31, 2023 20:00.

When John got home, he copied all his encrypted documentation files to the hidden memory of the new device. Next, he loaded some of his program files, photos, pictures, and general documents onto the solid-state drive.

John and Rhonda had started attending a local church shortly after they moved to the area. The church was having a fall festival. John and Rhonda decided to swing by and see the festivities. Rhonda was visiting with a friend from their Sunday School class. John was in line to get them some hotdogs. Suddenly someone behind him called his name. John recognized him immediately. It was Jeff Gray from high school. John had lost touch with most of his classmates. John and Jeff visited for a while and exchanged phone numbers. They tentatively scheduled a lunch together the following Tuesday. John had always liked Jeff and remembered going to his house a few times as a kid between Sunday morning and evening services.

The following Tuesday they met at the East End Café. They talked about their families and careers. John was interested to learn that Jeff worked for the FBI, out of their Little Rock office. John told Jeff a little about his work as a part-time contractor for the CIA. As it turned out John and Jeff only lived about five miles apart. They talked about the violence in town and how it was spreading. After lunch they promised to keep in touch and plan another lunch soon.

The following week John was surprised when Jeff phoned him. Jeff asked John if he was free for lunch the following day. They met at Los Toritos, the local Mexican restaurant in East End. After they had ordered, Jeff asked John if he thought he might like to work for the FBI. John was caught off guard. Obviously, Jeff had already checked on John's background. John told Jeff he'd have to think about it. But at the moment, John thought he'd had enough of working with the government for a while. Jeff understood and offered to give John a brief tour of the FBI's facilities in Little Rock. John accepted and they drove to Little Rock after lunch.

The FBI building was surrounded by a security fence and key card gated entry points. Once they had checked in at the security desk, Jeff showed John a spacious lunchroom, a physical fitness workout room, there were numerous offices, backup generators, and security cameras everywhere. The place looked very nice and new despite the building being several years old. Jeff introduced John to several manager types and then the tour was over.

On the way back John asked Jeff about their computer systems and what types of cases Jeff worked on. Jeff didn't know much about the FBI's computer systems. But he didn't mind telling John about the types of cases he had worked on. The cases were a wide variety of types such as bank robberies, drugs, counterfeit money, and illegal guns. They had data from most state and federal databases to pull from. John briefly told Jeff about the AI computer system he got to use at the CIA. Jeff had no idea if the FBI had anything like that.

Two weeks later Jeff and John ate lunch at East End Café again. This time Jeff brought a coworker. Bill Lewis was introduced to John as an FBI computer guy. Bill corrected Jeff and told John he was actually a computer data analyst. John and Bill immediately hit it off. Bill was very interested in the type of computer applications John had developed. John told him about the Prophet X program and developing the cryptographic system for the CIA. It was rare to get to talk to someone who actually appreciated the complexity of his program development. Jeff was feeling like a third wheel after a while. Most of what Bill and John talked about just sounded like a bunch of gibberish to him.

John had forgotten how nice it was to work with other computer programmers. It had been so long since John had been around coworkers that actually understood what he was doing. Jeff had indicated that the FBI was looking for a part-timer to help with their computer systems. It sounded like a fun alternative to the things he had been doing for the CIA.

Several weeks later John phoned McGuire.

"Hello John. Ready to be a productive citizen again?"

"Hello Mr. McGuire. I'll be brief. I know you're busy. I ran into an old classmate here in East End and he offered me a job. Before I committed to anything I wanted to pass it by you first."

"I'm flattered. Who would you be working for?"

"The FBI here in Arkansas."

"John, I hate to tell you this, but we have a gentleman's agreement with the FBI. We don't hire their people and they don't hire ours."

"I suspected as much. I was just a contractor for the CIA, not a real employee. Does that make a difference?"

"I doubt it will make any difference."

John had considered a negative response and had prepared for resistance from the CIA.

"McGuire, do you remember that documentation I have of our first meetings?"

"Yes."

"What if I agreed to turn it all over to you. Would that change the situation with me working for the FBI?"

"I think we could make that work."

"If you can get me approved to work for the FBI and they hire me, then I'll give you all the documentation I have. Is it a deal?"

"I can't make any promises. Give me a few days to work on it. It will take time to get this approved. I will call you when I know something. Was there anything else?"

"No sir. That's all I need for now."

They said goodbye and hung up.

A few weeks later John was working on a new application for the utility company. It was about 9:30 that morning when someone rang the doorbell. Rhonda was visiting her mother and dad, in Benton. John opened the door and there was a guy in a suit at the door. He introduced himself as Officer McDaniels of the FBI. He asked if he could come in. John showed him into the living room, and they sat down. The officer placed his briefcase on the coffee table and removed several documents from it. As he handed them to John he said, "Mr. Davidson, I've been sent to hopefully get your signature on a few documents. Take your time. Read them over carefully. The documents must remain in my sight. You're under no obligation to sign anything."

John started scanning the documents. The first one was an application for hire from the FBI. The next one was a consent to a background check and the last document was a confidentiality agreement. All of the data fields had been filled in for him. All that was required was his signature. Apparently, someone had already looked up all this data on him. They had his schooling, work history, relatives, home address, even his social security number. After making sure all the data was correct, he signed the documents and handed them back to Officer McDaniels.

"What happens now?"

"Sir I'm just here to get the papers signed. I don't make the decisions. But I can tell you that it normally takes four to six weeks to get all of the required background checks finished."

"Four to six weeks?"

"Welcome to the government. Things move very slowly in the office according to different departments, budget constraints, red tape, yada-yada-yada. Plus, these background checks are very thorough. They will check your credit history, your bank accounts, criminal history, travel outside the country, known associations, family members, everything. It all takes a while. Well, I need to be heading back to the office and get these forms turned in."

As they walked to the door John said, "Be safe. Maybe I'll see you again in a month or so."

"Perhaps. Have a good day."

After watching the blue government sedan back out of his driveway, John wrote down the date and time, the guy's name, license plate number, car and physical description, and a description of the forms he had signed. He filed the paper scrap in a folder and went back to work on the new application he was developing. He needed to add some tables to the database this application would use for data storage. It was midafternoon before he knew it.

The phone rang. It was Jeff Gray. "Hello, Jeff. What's up?"

"There are a few guys here in the office that would like to meet you. I was wondering if you might be available tomorrow morning?"

"Sure. What time."

"If you could be here around ten in the morning, that would work great."

"OK, I'll be there, but how will I get in?"

"Use the button on the intercom at the gate. Tell the security officer your name and that you're here to see me. They will let you in. Park and I'll meet you at the front door."

"Sounds good. I'll see you in the morning."

The next morning John got ready and drove into town (Little Rock). When he walked up to the main entrance, Jeff was there to let him in. The first stop after getting his visitors badge was to be introduced to Mr. McKenzie. He was the Director of operations.

"Hello Mr. Davidson. Nice to finally meet you. Jeff tells me you will be a valuable asset to our office."

"Well, I guess that remains to be seen. I hope to help where I can."

"Mr. McGuire had a lot of complementary things to say about you. He couldn't go into details. But I understand you are uniquely gifted in problem solving."

"I'm sure Mr. McGuire embellished the truth a lot in that regard."

"Come, come, Mr. Davidson. Don't be so modest. While we are separate branches of the government, word does spread about unusual assets."

"I'm afraid this asset may disappoint you. But my wife would whole-heartedly agree on the unusual part. I'm nothing special. I just get lucky sometimes."

That word 'lucky'. It was bitter in John's mouth as soon as he said it. He knew he had only prospered because he was blessed by God.

"Well, I guess we will see if that good luck followed you here from the beach. Nice to meet you."

The next stop, and John's favorite, was to the FBI computer lab. He saw Bill Lewis and was introduced to the rest of the computer team. He met Jill Stephens. She was Bill Lewis' boss and the manager of the computer lab. He could have spent the rest of the day talking to these guys about programming. But after about 30 minutes, John noticed Jeff was getting a little bored. So, he said his goodbyes and they left the computer lab.

They had a quick lunch in the cafeteria and then Jeff took John to the indoor gun range. At the desk John was issued a 10mm pistol, a box of ammunition and hearing protectors. This was a typical indoor gun range, except the walls were specially constructed to totally cancel all noise. In the adjacent rooms no one ever heard a gunshot. John did very well at the twenty-five-yard range. He didn't know it at the time, but this was his qualification test on the range. After that Jeff ran the targets out to fifty yards. Jeff's ten shots were fairly scattered. John had significantly tightened his grouping after the second shot.

"Wow! John did you say you shot with a 10mm before?"

"Not until today. Why?"

"Nothing. Great shooting."

"Thank you. Just beginner's luck, I guess."

There was that word again, 'luck'. It still left a bitter taste in his mouth. Then he added. "God has always been good to me".

Later that afternoon, after John had left, Jeff reported John's shooting range scores to the director, Mr. McKenzie.

Chapter 13

The following Sunday after Bible study in the 'Truth Seekers's class, Mr. and Mrs. Halpine introduced themselves. Lewis Halpine was the class teacher. They all seemed to hit it off and agreed to eat Sunday lunch together at the local Mexican diner, Los Toritos, after church.

At the dinner they found they had a lot in common in terms of age, families, and upbringing. They had a great time eating and getting to know each other. By the end of the meal, they were fast friends and promised to get together again soon.

After they got home that evening, they did what most married couples do, they discussed the sermon, the Bible lesson, and the Halpines.

"John, what did you think of Lewis?"

"I really like him. He grew up around here. But, we had basically the same childhood; just different careers. He knows a lot of neat stuff about mechanical engineering. He and Karen were married just two years after we were. Did you know he was a manager?"

"No. But that Karen is crazy in a good way. She's so much fun to be around. I really like her. They do a lot of things at the church."

"I think we should plan to spend some more time with them."

"Definitely."

The following Thursday Mr. McGuire phoned John and invited him to a luncheon in Houston. John initially declined. But McGuire was able to talk him into coming. McGuire's administrative assistant, Sue, made the travel arrangements and purchased the airline tickets from

Little Rock to Houston and rental car for the following Thursday. She forwarded the travel itinerary to John via his email.

Thursday morning John boarded a plane at Little Rock International Airport. During the flight it occurred to him that he had no idea what this luncheon was about. He wondered if he was somehow being snookered by the CIA again. No sense in worrying about that now. He was pretty much committed to whatever it was.

After landing at Bush International airport, John got his rental car and drove to the restaurant. He arrived at Landry's Seafood Restaurant in The Woodlands a little before noon. The strange thing was that this was about forty-five minutes from the Houston CIA offices.

When he arrived, Mike Lambert greeted him at the front desk and showed him to a large table in the rear of the restaurant. In a few minutes a lot of the people he had met in the CIA offices drifted in. And then, to his surprise some of his coworkers from the utility company also joined them. Don McCarthy, his utility company boss, was there as well. He was pleasantly surprised. He couldn't understand why all these people were here together. There were two large tables of people, most of them from the CIA, maybe 20 people all together.

After they had all ordered and received their drinks McGuire stood to make an announcement.

"May I have your attention for a moment please… We are here to honor a valued member of our team, John Davidson. John has proven to be invaluable to us all in many ways. I cannot speak directly about his contributions to the utility company. However, I can tell you he has been a valuable asset to our teams in the government. It is with some regret we have allowed John to leave our government office. I understand he is still working for the local utility to help keep our lights on, and for that we are also much obliged."

With that McGuire raised his tea glass in a toast to John.

John was beyond embarrassed. He was utterly speechless. So, he stood and said, "Thank you. But I think you have the wrong John Davidson." To that all of CIA and a few of the utility folks laughed.

"Seriously. I have been privileged and blessed to work with most of you in my career. I hope we might still have the opportunity to work together in the future. As for my so-called value, I'd have to say that Mr. McGuire's estimation of my value is grossly overestimated. Just ask my wife." More laughing ensued.

"Seriously, thank you all for putting up with me. That is a talent I thought only my wife possessed."

John sat down and everyone clapped. The CIA picked up the tab for the dinner. John enjoyed getting to visit with many people he hadn't seen in a while. One in particular was Luke Morgan. John always felt bad about how Luke had stumbled across one of the rogue programs he had written. The program had done exactly what John had intended. It had identified and penalized the person trying to steal the Prophet X program. At the time, Luke was a new field agent on his first ever field mission. He had tried to rush in and steal a copy of John's program. When he ran the program on his CIA laptop, it sent an Email to John and destroyed all the data and then the operating system on his computer. Luke had almost lost his job at the CIA over that. John had always felt bad for him.

As people were starting to leave and go back to the office, Don McCarthy, his utility company boss, hung back. After most of the people had left, he shook John's hand and said, "Glad you could make it." They laughed. Then Don said, "John, don't tell anyone, but I'm retiring in three weeks. I mailed my retirement papers in yesterday." John was shocked. Don was by far the best boss he had ever worked for.

"Man, if you're leaving then I guess that means we all need to be looking for another job."

"No, it's just time for me to move on."

"Why now?"

"John, it's just not the same company anymore. Most of us old timers are leaving and making room for the new guys."

"I think you told me as much the last time we talked. Don, I want to say it one more time. You're the best boss I've ever had. Thanks for everything."

"John, it's not every day the CIA invites a utility employee and his buddies to lunch on the government's tab. None of us know what you did for them. But I can guarantee everyone in the office is talking about it. Maybe someday you'll tell me about it?"

John looked down at the floor. "Well, sure, I can tell you... But then, I'd have to kill you."

They both had a chuckle.

"Don, I can tell you I took them somewhere they didn't want to go. I forced them to kiss me or kill me. If they had chosen to kill me, I made sure it was going to cost them. I am so blessed that they chose to kiss and make-up instead. After that, I did a little work for them from time-to-time. I learned a lot in the process. It was a very interesting ride. But I jumped off that merry-go-round last week. That's what this lunch was about. I put the CIA in my rear-view last week. And to tell you the truth, I'm not sure how long I'll stay at the utility company now that you're leaving. Guess I'll see what my next boss is like before I decide."

Don said, "Keep the wind to your back."

They shook hands and left.

On the flight home John thought about what Don had said and wondered if he too should be considering leaving the utility company.

Chapter 14

~

A few weeks later John was introduced to his new boss at the utility company on a phone conference. A few weeks later his new boss sent him and email informing him that he would need to be in the Woodlands office a minimum of three days a week. John was not specifically asked to respond to the email and no specific date was given for when this would be expected to occur. So, John had a few days to pray and think about his response. Just as Don had said, the utility company was changing. Hard work, loyalty, dedication, and proven skills were no longer desirable qualities in the work force. They were much more focused on social and minority issues than building a more reliable and efficient utility system. The new management seemed to despise the workers who had worked hard and made sacrifices to make the company profitable and strong. They demanded the right to micromanage every aspect of the work. No room for creativity. Perhaps, John thought, his season at the utility company was coming to a close.

A month later John phoned the utility company's Human Resources department, requested a copy of his retirement benefits, and resigned from the utility company.

The day he filed his retirement papers he phoned Don. He agreed to come to Kenner, Louisiana to visit within the next few months.

Mike phoned two days before John's official last day at the utility company. He told John that he, Linda, and the girls were going to be passing through Little Rock on the way to Branson, Missouri. He asked if John might be available to eat Lunch with them in Little

Rock the following day. John said yes. They would meet at the Cracker Barrel restaurant, and he would bring Rhonda. At lunch Mike told John about the investigation over the trap John and McGuire had set. Apparently, they had discovered someone in one of the accounting department was selling classified information. Internal affairs had gotten involved and there was talk about a government oversite committee investigation. It was going to be a big messy investigation. Everyone was going to be interviewed and polygraphed.

"Gee Mike, aren't you glad you retired."

"John, I have to go in for an interview like everyone else. I'm surprised they haven't called you in yet."

"But I was just a contractor."

"You had access to the computers and databases."

"Wow, I didn't think of it that way. You really think they will be calling me?"

"Yes. They're going to use this as an excuse for a witch hunt."

"I been meaning to ask you. Would you like to go deer hunting with me in November?"

"Absolutely! Send me the dates and I'll be there. But you'll have to coach me some. I've never been deer hunting before."

"No problem."

They finished a long lunch and said their goodbyes.

John sure hoped they didn't call him in. He had nothing to hide. But still, they could ask a lot of questions. Some of them John might not really want to answer.

Jeff Gray phoned late Friday afternoon. It had been almost a month since they last spoke.

"Hi John. How was your week?"

"It's been pretty boring since I resigned from the utility company."

"Maybe I can help you with that. They want to offer you a full-time job."

"What happened to the part-time job?"

"Well, it came to our attention that you have recently become unemployed. We thought you might prefer better pay, benefits, all that stuff. But the part-time job is still there as well."

"I see. OK, how much time will I have to spend in the office each week. I've become a very productive remote access worker over the past few years."

"They will want you in the office forty hours for the first few weeks. After that, they should let you work from home a few days a week. It depends on what they need from you."

"What will I be doing?"

"It's that computer stuff you like, that's all I know."

"OK. Sounds good. When do I start?"

"A week from next Monday at 8:00. I'll meet you at the front entrance again."

After hanging up John realized that he was now starting a new career. It seemed like the changes were still coming. At this rate there was no telling where things would end up. He was both anxious and excited that God seemed to be moving him towards something, some place, some person. He thought it was probably a good time to spend some time alone. Not exactly alone. He needed a quiet place, with no distraction, and time to pray and ask for God's guidance.

Chapter 15

~

After discussing it with Rhonda, John phoned and reserved a cabin in northern Arkansas. Before leaving the pavement, they stopped by the owner's house to sign in. They had known Jim Pearson Jr. for over thirty years. He and his miniature collie Warwick greeted them. Then, they headed down the long pasture road that led to the canyon.

This was a special place. Rhonda and John had been here many times. It was a unique place tucked away in a canyon. The Bushmaster cabin was built over one of the two creeks that flowed into the canyon. It was a remote area; so remote that there was no need for curtains on the windows. A goat would have to hike the canyons and mountains for about 4 miles to get to this place. Any restaurant or grocery store was a thirty to forty five-minute drive away. There was no traffic noise. The only sounds to be heard were those of the birds and breezes rushing through the treetops. There were no phones and cellular phones didn't work down in the canyon. There was no TV and all but a few of the local radio stations tended to fade in and out due to nightfall or bad weather. It was a place to be away from distractions. A place to reflect and reconnect with your spouse. There were no agendas, schedules, or timetables here. The sun was your clock. It was hard to spend more than a day here and not be awestruck by the beauty of God's creation.

While hiking the gravel road or trails it was not uncommon to see squirrels, deer and eagles soaring high above the tree canopy. Over the years they had seen deer, coyotes, fox, bobcats, and lots of other creatures. At night they always looked forward to seeing the ever-present racoon family eating the dry dog food they would leave on the deck, just outside the glass door.

They could only stay four days. The cabin was already booked after that. Normally they tried to stay a week. But they hadn't planned ahead this time. It was great falling asleep to the sound of running water in the stream under the cabin, sleeping in, reading books, playing card games, and hiking the canyon trails. They had occasionally spent an entire week here and never seen another person.

The nights dipped below freezing and by lunch it would be well above sixty degrees. Perfect for hiking or lying in a hammock. This year the fangs were long. That's what they called the ice sickles that hung from the cliffs in the canyon. They would sometimes fall during the night and shatter on the canyon floor. On one of their previous stays the canyon's waterfall had frozen. That year there had been ice and snow all over the canyon. It made the steep climb out a challenge for any vehicle.

The second evening, they were coming back to the cabin from a long hike and met a couple on the road. They were staying in the only other cabin in this canyon. This was their first visit to the Longbow resort. Their names were Andy and Sheryl Duhon. They had driven up from Louisiana for a few nights. John told them where most of the trails were and places they liked to hike.

The temperatures were dropping and the third night they heard the sleet hitting the tin roof of the cabin. By the morning the sleet had stopped and there was a thin coat of ice on everything. The ice wouldn't last long. By midday the intermittent sun and sixty-five-degree temperatures had melted everything.

The days went by far too quickly up here and soon it was time to pack up and leave this slice of heaven in the canyon. The time alone, the solitude, the peaceful forest, it had all been such a welcome time to commune with God. On the road back to civilization their phones started picking up all the messages and emails they had missed.

In November Mike Lambert flew from Mobile to Little Rock. John picked him up at the airport. Rhonda had the guest room prepared. Dinner was burgers on the grill with French fries. After dinner they retired early. John had loaded his Rubicon Jeep up with everything they would need for their hunting trip. They got up before daybreak and left for deer camp. As they were leaving Mike suddenly had a bunch of questions.

"Don't I need a gun to hunt with?"

"I have one for you."

"What about a hunting license?"

"We'll stop at Walmart, and you can buy one there."

It sounded like John had everything covered. So, Mike started to relax.

After a stop at Walmart, they drove south and eventually left the pavement for some timber company roads. Eventually they came to a clearing with several trailers and a cook tent setup. The cooking tent had tables, a gas stove, two refrigerators and a barrel stove in the back. This was where they ate their meals and sat around the barrel stove after dinner. There was a trailer that John and Mike would use. It belonged to one of the hunting club members that couldn't make it for opening week.

John introduced Mike to the other hunting club members. After they got their gear in the trailer, John showed Mike a topographical map of the area. He showed Mike where they were and where they would be hunting the next morning. John warned Mike that they would need to be on the stands before daybreak and would not come in until noon. Next John got out the rifles. He had his 243 and then he had an identical 243 that had belonged to his dad. He briefed Mike on the features of the rifle and made sure Mike understood. Next, he tossed Mike an orange vest and orange cap. These were required for safety in the woods this time of year.

John tried to tell Mike the basics of hunting from a stand. He told Mike to get in a comfortable position, relax, and just be still as a statue for as long as he could while listening for a deer walking through the leaves and to try and only move his eyes.

Mike was concerned about finding the deer hunting stand in the dark. John assured him that he would walk him into the stand before continuing on to his own stand. Lastly, John gave Mike a small walkie talkie. It would allow Mike to call John if he shot a deer or needed help for some reason.

The next morning at 04:00 they got up and got dressed. The coffee and breakfast were ready when they got to the cooking tent. They had coffee, scrambled eggs, toast, sausage patties and white gravy. After breakfast they grabbed some water bottles and snacks and headed for the trailer. In a matter of minutes, they had all their gear loaded and were driving down the timber company road. At a wide spot in the road John pulled over and stopped. They got their stuff out of the Rubicon and John handed Mike a flashlight. They walked down a path through the woods until John abruptly turned to the left and walked out through the woods for about 100 yards and stopped. He pointed his flashlight at a ladder that had suddenly appeared on the side of a tree. Except this was not a tree. It was one of four legs of a deer stand. John pointed out the four-foot square above them. It had heavy felt hanging around the rails. Then John pointed his flashlight first in one direction and then another. He whispered to Mike "These are the shooting lanes where you're likely to get a shot at a deer. There is an old swivel office chair up in the stand. If you need anything use the radio. I will come back by here around noon to pick you up." Mike whispered, "Got it. See you around noon." With that Mike slung the rifle over his shoulder and started up the ladder.

John walked back out to the trail and continued on for another two thousand yards before turning into the woods and finding his deer stand. As he sat there, he couldn't help but remember all of the hunting trips with his father. He had been hunting since he was about eleven years old. Before too long the sky started to lighten up and then it was daybreak. The woods slowly came to life with the birds and squirrels. It was relaxing to just sit and watch nature. Soon he heard something approaching from the rear. There were two doe deer browsing and moving under the deer stand. They had no idea he was there just seven feet above them. He watched as they browsed and passed down one of the shooting lanes. They seemed to be rushed. Soon he saw why. There was a nice ten-point buck following them. He was smart. He stayed out of the shooting lane and behind bushes and trees. But John saw him slipping off in the same direction the two does had just gone. He would have to cross through the shooting lane to continue following the doe. He stopped behind a big tree for a long few seconds and then, he stepped out into the shooting lane. John had gotten his gun braced on the shooting rail and had a good shot. At 110 yards it was an easy shot. John placed the bullet just above the shoulder of the deer. The shot dropped the buck right where he had stood.

Mike was watching two gray squirrels chasing each other when the shot made him jump. There was the characteristic pop and then a large boom. He had heard John explain it, but to hear it was something else.

The squirrels ran up to the tree canopy. All the wood noises had just returned when Mike heard something walking in the leaves to his left. He cut his eyes but couldn't see anything. He remained frozen until the noise sounded like it was almost under his stand. He peaked over the rail. There was a six-point buck right under his stand. He got the gun up on the rail and waited on the deer to walk away from the stand. After a few minutes the buck started moving towards a stand of trees. The deer turned to the left and stopped. Mike took aim and fired. The deer jumped, wheeled, and bolted for the cover of the forest. Mike heard the deer fall just out of his site. Mike grabbed the radio.

"I shot one."

"I heard. Stay in your stand. Keep hunting. I'll be back up there in a little while. I'll be the one in orange. Don't shoot me!"

"OK. Should I go find the deer I shot?"

"Did you hear him fall, or did he run away?"

"I heard him fall just a little ways into the woods."

"Sounds like you got him. Just stay on the stand. I'll be there in a little while."

John had cut through the woods, and circled well away from Mike and went back to the road. He took the Rubicon back to camp and got on a friend's four-wheeler. In about 30 minutes he was pulling up to the stand Mike was on.

"Where is he?"

"I shot him over here and he fell over there." Mike pointed.

John saw where the deer was standing when Mike shot it. They walked about 50 yards and found the deer. John pulled the four-wheeler over, and they loaded the deer up.

"Tag the deer. We'll take it back to camp and then I'll come get the one I shot."

After they had both deer back at camp, they loaded them into the rear of a pick-up truck and headed to a local meat processor.

"What did you think about your first deer hunt?"

"I was pumped when I took that shot. I was afraid I would miss."

"Was the deer standing still when you shot?"

"Yes."

"Nice shot. It looks like you placed it well. Obviously good enough."

"What about the one you shot?"

"Yes, he was standing still when I shot."

"Was he close in, like mine?"

"No. He was maybe 120 yards out when I shot. It's still a pretty close shot for these guns. I usually hunt on the timber company road and get longer shots. I have the guns zeroed in at 200 yards. That's why I told you to aim for the middle of the deer's shoulder. I have taken most of my deer at 350 or more yards. I'll send you my deer meat chili recipe. Linda and the girls will love it. I also have one for barbeque deer meat sandwiches. It's one of our favorites."

Mike was beginning to see why John preferred the long guns. They were excellent tools for hunting.

"Where did you learn how to skin a deer?"

"Right here. At that same skinning station, we used today. My dad made sure I knew everything about harvesting deer. But, now days, it's easier to just get someone else to process and package the meat. It gets us back on the deer stand quicker."

The rest of the week they continued to hunt, and Mike found he loved hearing the hunting stories of times past. The guys loved retelling the old stories of days long gone by. He soon discovered the same thing that most deer hunters do. Hunting was a time to slow down. A time to think and consider your life choices. A time to appreciate nature and watch a spider build a web. All the while, your mind settles and becomes at peace.

After the meat was processed, John would store the meat in his freezer until he could take it to Mike.

They drove back to John's house after the last day's hunt. They got cleaned up and went out to dinner in Little Rock. John had tagged out and Mike had managed to bag two deer. The next morning John took Mike to the airport for his flight back to Mobile.

Chapter 16

~

At the FBI computer lab John had his first real assignment. He had been given five names and was asked to pull all the data he could from the various databases on each name. Pulling the data was the easy part. Filtering out unwanted data and finding where the five people may have crossed paths would be the tedious time-consuming part.

There had to be a better way. Sounded like a good way to get to know a few of his new co-workers. He went to Susan Terry's office and asked her for pointers on how she would put all of the data together. She had been in the computer lab for three years and should know some shortcuts. She showed him how she manually deleted unwanted data and then manually went through the reports to find common points between the subjects. She was meticulous and thorough in her work. John thanked her for the help and went back to his desk.

John built a few custom queries that seemed to eliminate most of the unwanted data and dumped the result of the query into a custom table he had created. Then he built a custom query to run against the new table and report any matching data between the subjects.

It took John two days to get the queries to run smoothly. But man did this save a lot of time. The last thing he needed was to develop a reporting tool to put all the data in a logical format. He developed a formatted input file that the queries used to search the various databases.

By noon Friday, John finally had the program running like he wanted. He generated a final report and sent it to Jill Stephens (his boss) for validation before it was sent back to the requestor. He suspected she would want him to make some changes to the final report. He had no idea how these reports were supposed to look.

Around 2:30 Jill stuck her head into John's office door. "Got a minute?"

"Sure. I figured you would have some changes for me."

"Well yes, a few minor changes. But I wanted to ask you who helped you pull this data together?"

"Everyone was pretty busy. So, I just sort of did the best I could."

"I see. I should have had someone work with you and show you the ropes. But this is very good work. I'll show you how to format the reports. But the data looks good to me. Can you give me a copy of the data you took out of the report?"

"Yes. I'll need a few minutes."

"I can wait." She wanted to see him work.

He had written all the erroneous, duplicate, and unwanted data into a separate table in his initial queries. He used this to make sure his queries were not deleting good data from the output. He pulled the data from the tables and printed the twenty-page report out on the laser printer in his office.

Jill scanned through the data. After a few minutes she asked, "How did you separate this data out of the query?"

John explained the custom queries he had created. He wasn't sure how much of it Jill understood. But she acted like she did.

She suggested that he add the culled data as an appendix to the original report. There was a standard header they wanted on each section of the report. These were minor changes. John made the changes and emailed the new report to Jill.

The next similar request he got would be done in hours not days.

Wednesday of the following week, Jill asked John what he thought it would take to build an AI based computer system for the FBI and what benefits they would get from it. John told her he could help in the development of an AI based server, but as to the benefits, it just depended on how they might want to use it. Jill told him she was thinking about adding it to next year's budget and might want to talk to him some more later.

Thursday started off cloudy and the clouds built steadily through the day. Just as everyone was leaving work the clouds started to take on a dark foreboding look. By the time John got home he noticed the wind had turned cooler and the dark clouds were moving in opposite directions. Not a good sign. This meant that there were two weather fronts colliding. John went inside and turned the television to a local news station. There were tornado watches issued for central Arkansas. Their house was in one of the current tornado watch boxes on the weather radar. The weatherman was indicating some circular motion on the doppler radar just north of their house. John went to tell Rhonda, in her home office. Before he got down the hallway, he heard the tornado warning sirens go off. There was really very little to do in the face of a direct tornado hit. If you had a reinforced safe room or a tornado shelter, then that was the place to go. But for Rhonda and John the best place was their pantry or possibly one of the cars in the garage.

A tornado could easily produce two hundred mile per hour winds. At those speeds a telephone pole, uprooted tree or limb becomes a projectile traveling at over one hundred miles per hour. It easily penetrates and demolishes almost anything it hits. The only good thing about tornados was that they normally didn't stay on the ground long. The path of devastation was typically several hundred yards wide and ran for less than a mile. But in that swath the devastation is massive. Nothing is left standing. That is why most storm shelters are built below ground.

An hour later the tornado warnings had been lifted and all that remained was gusty wind with a driven rain. There was still a little hail on the sidewalk. But these hail stones were far too small to cause any damage. As they watched the news, they learned that North Little

Rock had taken a direct hit. There were cars blown over and buildings with the roofs ripped off. The electricity was out for a huge part of the area. It would take several days to get the streets cleared of debris and have the power restored.

The following morning John was notified via email that the FBI office in Little Rock would be closed to allow employees to focus on helping to rebuild the devastated communities in and around Little Rock.

Friday evening John and Rhonda went to eat with the Halpines. They had agreed to meet at the Cracker Barrel restaurant in Bryant, Arkansas. As they arrived at the restaurant, they spotted the Halpines sitting at a table near the back. They made their way over and were greeted with big hugs and smiles. There was another couple at the table. Lewis introduced them to Kevin and Patricia Baxley. The Baxleys were about ten years younger than the Halpines and Davidsons. The waitress came and took everyone's order. As they waited for their food, they reminisced about old times and talked about their families. The conversation flowed easily, and before they knew it, their meals had arrived. Everyone dug in, enjoying the delicious southern fare and swapping stories between bites.

The atmosphere at the Cracker Barrel was warm and welcoming, with the sound of country music softly playing in the background. The restaurant was decorated with relics from a long past American decor, which made for a cozy and nostalgic setting.

John learned that Kevin worked for a local heating and air conditioning company. He had attended church almost all his life. He lived in Spring Lake subdivision, about three miles from the Davidson's house. They were from south Texas, about thirty miles from where John and Rhonda had lived.

As the evening progressed the conversation turned to last Sunday's sermon. Kevin Baxley's Bible knowledge impressed John. It was not often he was around such people, and he really enjoyed the company. Kevin had heard about Bible codes and knew a little about the Prophet X program John had written. Out of habit John tried to change the subject. He didn't like being the center of attention.

John: "So, have you guys seen any good movies lately?"

Kevin: "Yeah, I saw a pretty good one last week. But I was really interested in hearing more about Prophet X. Why didn't you sell it?"

Now Lewis and Kevin were both asking him questions about the Prophet X program. John tried to limit his answers to short responses. But that only led to more questions. After dinner and a million questions about Prophet X each of the couples shared a dessert and finally said their good-byes.

On the way home John and Rhonda decided they really liked the Baxley's and would need to have them over for dinner sometime.

Amanda had been looking forward to coming home from college for the weekend. She missed her family, her bed, and the familiarity of home. As soon as she parked in the driveway, she felt a sense of relief wash over her.

John and Rhonda were waiting for her at the front door, and they hugged her tightly. Amanda smiled, feeling their love and warmth. They chatted as they walked into the house, catching up on each other's news.

As she stepped into the house, Amanda breathed in the familiar scents of home. Later she could hear her father's voice in the kitchen as he prepared dinner, and the clanging of pots and pans. Her mom had started washing the two bags of dirty clothes Amanda had brought home from college.

Amanda spent the weekend catching up with her family, laughing at old memories, and enjoying home-cooked food. She went on a long walk with her mother, sharing her college experiences and her plans for the future. She played card games with her mother and watched movies with her father.

Sunday morning, Amanda and her family attended church services before she headed back to school. As they said their goodbyes, Amanda felt grateful for the weekend with her loved ones and hopeful for the future. She realized that her faith and family would always be a source of strength and support, no matter where life might take her.

Chapter 17

~

The following Wednesday when John got to the FBI computer lab there was a message taped to his office door. It said he needed to call Mr. McKenzie (Director of Operations) a.s.a.p.. Mr. McKenzie's administrative assistant answered the phone and told John that Mr. McKenzie was free at the moment and wanted to see him. A few minutes later, John knocked on Mr. McKenzie's door.

"John! Please come in and shut the door."

"You wanted to see me?"

"Yes, I wanted to ask you about your training in the CIA. I know you didn't participate in field work. But did they give you any training?"

"Yes. I had field operations training at camp Peary."

"I only ask because an opportunity has come up. It's a task I feel you are uniquely suited for. I'll need you to keep this quiet. Because a lot of guys in this office are going to be upset that they didn't get asked."

John figured the hook would be coming soon and Mr. McKenzie was just baiting the hook.

"John, I understand you and Rhonda like to SCUBA dive. Is that right?"

"Yes." and John thought here comes the hook...

"Are your diving certifications still good?"

"Yes."

"We would like to send you and Rhonda on a little SCUBA diving vacation to the Cayman Islands. I understand the diving there is quite spectacular."

"Yes. As you know we have been there once before."

"Well, the government will pay for everything. We just need you to do a little favor for us. You will be given a memory stick at the Grand

Cayman Island airport. Bring it back here and that's it. The whole week is yours to enjoy, on us. What do you say?"

"Can we stay at Little Cayman Beach Resort for the week?"

"Sure, no problem. Is that in Grand Cayman?"

"No. We will take a small puddle jumper off Grand Cayman Island to Little Cayman Island. It will get us clear of anybody looking for us in Grand Cayman. It's a small island, a preferred SCUBA diving destination, and they have some spectacular sunsets there. A lot less people too."

"Sounds reasonable. See Sally on the way out and tell her what you need. This needs to happen in two weeks. Is that a problem?"

"No problem. I'm sure we can get our gear sorted out by then."

"Wait a sec. You do have all the SCUBA equipment already, right?"

"Yes, we have all the SCUBA gear at the house. I just need to get the regs serviced. I was going to have that done before our next dive."

"Good. I need you to look over this operations file. We want you to be fully aware of all the parameters of this operation."

Mr. McKenzie slid a manila folder across his desk for John to read. There were only three pages in the folder. The first two were emails between Mr. McKenzie and people John didn't know. The third page detailed the operation. The case was code named 'Receiver'. Some guy would approach John at The Grand Cayman airport and give him a memory stick. John would carry an air tag to allow the contact to find him. The contact would ask him if he lived on Grand Cayman. John would respond "Not for the past twelve years." Simple.

John slid the folder back to Mr. McKenzie.

"Where do I get this air tag from?"

"Sally will give it to you next week. Any questions or concerns?"

"No. Sounds easy."

"Good. Remember to not tell anyone here about this. OK?"

"No problem."

John left Mr. McKenzie office and sat down at Sally's desk to make the travel arrangements."

Early Saturday morning found John and Rhonda at the Little Rock airport. They each had a backpack and a carryon. The rest of the dive gear was in a single checked bag. John placed the air tag in his backpack. John had been preparing their equipment for the past two weeks. He had charged all the batteries for the cameras, dive lights and dive computers. He had lubricated all of the seals with silicone grease to ensure all of the equipment was watertight. Everything was checked and re-checked before packing.

It would be a full day of airports and flights from this point on. After a transfer at the Dallas-Fort Worth airport they finally arrived at Grand Cayman airport around noon. John and Rhonda had three hours to kill awaiting the small puddle jumper flight to Little Cayman Island. John left Rhonda near the boarding area and walked to a relatively abandoned sitting area. He didn't have to wait long. A thirty-something guy, in shorts and a tee-shirt, with a dark complexion came and sat a few seats away. After checking his phone for a few minutes, the guy asked, "You live here in Grand Cayman?"

John responded, "Not for the past twelve years."

The guy bent down by John's backpack, as if to pick something up off the floor.

"Is this yours?"

"Thank you."

John took the memory stick and shoved it into a pocket of his backpack.

After a few more minutes, the guy got up and left the sitting area. John stayed there another fifteen minutes, sipping a coffee, surfing the internet, and then gathered his stuff and went back to sit with Rhonda.

They had a three hour wait on the puddle jumper flight. When the boarding time finally came, they stood and got in line to walk out on the tarmac and board the plane. After taking their seats, John noticed that same thirty-something guy taking a seat. He was either going to Little Cayman or Brac island. John didn't like the coincidence. But there was nothing he could do about it. It was after three and they hadn't had breakfast or lunch. After flying all day, dinner and stretching out on a bed was starting to sound pretty good.

Once they arrived at the Little Cayman Beach Resort, they were checked-in and quickly found their room. It was a clean, modest room with two beds and a bathroom with a shower. There were plenty of plugins to charge cellular phones, batteries, and miscellaneous items. The air conditioning felt good as the weather was warm and humid outside. The rooms were located facing a freshwater swimming pool with a deck and chairs that looked out over the glistening waves of the ocean.

After a quick check-in with the dive shop it was time for dinner. All meals were included and served buffet style. They both decided on roasted chicken, mashed potatoes, green beans, and bread. For dessert they had a strawberry Jell-O and whip cream dish. The food was very good. They ate a quick dinner and returned to their room. John wanted to get all the dive gear lined out for the morning dive. He laid out their buoyancy control devices (BCDs), swim fins and dive masks. After that, he checked the dive computers, underwater cameras, and dive lights. Then he jotted a few notes in their travel log. A good night's sleep was needed as they had to be at the dock at seven-thirty for their first SCUBA dive the next morning. John powered up his laptop and sent an encrypted update to McKenzie's email address at the CIA.

The message was short, "Contact made at Grand Cayman airport. I have the memory stick. Contact boarded plane with us to Little Cayman Island." John ran this through the encryption tool using the password 'Receiver' from the case file and sent the email using the resorts Wi-Fi connection. He waited till the email program confirmed that the email had been sent, then he turned the laptop off and went to bed.

They slept well after the long travel day. The next morning John and Rhonda got up at six and went to the buffet. Then they went to their room and grabbed their dive gear and headed for the dock. As they were standing on the dock, waiting to board the dive boat, John found a familiar face. It was the contact from the airport at Grand Cayman. John had somehow missed seeing him get off the plane in Little Cayman. He was assigned to the same dive boat as John and Rhonda. This meant that they would be diving together all week. There were twelve divers and three crew members on the boat. John decided just to ignore the guy from the airport. The coincidence, if that's what it was, bothered him. But there wasn't anything he could do about it.

Seated on the dive boat next to John was an older man and woman. John introduced himself and Rhonda. The guy and lady were Annette and Carlos Hodges. They were brother and sister, and on a dive trip together.

The first dive was a relatively shallow reef dive at forty to sixty feet. They saw stingrays, nurse sharks, barracuda, and tons of tropical fish. The water temperature and clarity were perfect. It was like swimming in an aquarium full of tropical fish. As soon as they descended the mooring line to the sandy bottom, they practiced a few dive skills on the first few dives. The reefs and fish were beautiful. John had his underwater camera and was shooting photos of everything. He led the dives and Rhonda followed. They were careful to keep an eye on the other diver's bubble streams.

They had been swimming around the reef heads for about twenty minutes when John spotted an eagle ray swimming about one hundred feet away. These were majestic creatures with black skin and white circular spots all over. They flew gracefully without effort through the clear blue water. John kicked hard to close the distance while getting the camera set up for a good video. He was no match for the sea creature. But he did manage to stay within video distance long enough to get a short video.

After two dives the boat headed back to the resort. They had almost four hours before their afternoon dives. Over the course of the next few days, they dove every morning and evening. They saw eagle rays, turtles, sharks, lobster, moray eels, and many other aquatic species. The wall dive was spectacular. Just past the reef, the sea floor suddenly dropped vertically several thousand feet. It was like floating in space. All you could see below was darkness.

That night at dinner, John saw Annette and Carlos sitting at a nearby table. As they were eating John started to sense something was different about Annette and Carlos. It took him until the end of dinner to figure out what was off about them. They chose a table near the rear of the dining hall. They sat where they could easily see everyone in the room without looking suspicious. They were watching the people in the room. John decided to test a theory. He told Rhonda he would be right back. He went to the buffet and got a dessert and a coffee. But instead of stopping at the table where he and Rhonda had been eating, he went to an empty table to the rear and slightly behind the Hodges. As he sat down, he watched to see how the Hodges would react. It was very noticeable now that they had to crane their necks around and look over their shoulders to see John. These two were not just brother and sister on vacation. They were evaluating the people in the room, seldom looking at each other, and never missing any movement in the room. Very strange, John thought. After a few minutes John went back to the table where he had left Rhonda, and they went back to their room.

"What was that all about?" Rhonda asked John.

"There's something strange about that Annet and Carlos Hodges."

"What?"

"I'm not sure. But they seem off to me somehow. It's probably nothing."

Rhonda knew John felt uneasy around them for some reason.

On Tuesday morning's first dive they spotted a large sea turtle. It was busy plowing through the delicate coral and fans looking for something to eat. At some point it became interested in the divers. It charged Rhonda, but she was able to swim out of its way as John was snapping photos of the encounter. When it turned towards John, he paddled back away from it as best he could. It kept coming with its massively strong jaws working open and closed. John was able to swim up and over the turtle at the last minute. It continued off into the distance.

For the second dive that morning, the dive boat took them to Brac island, to dive on a shipwreck called the Tibbetts. The Tibbetts was a Russian war ship, with her original guns still in place. After she was deliberately sunk near the wall edge, a storm had pushed her back up into eighty feet of water and broke her in half. It was a very cool dive with tons of marine life all around it. The ship's guns made for some super great photos.

The dive boat was missing one of their divers. It was a guy that had sat towards the back of the boat on their short runs out to the dive sites. John couldn't remember the guy's name. But he remembered the guy had some old looking dive gear. John had wondered why he wasn't on the dive boat and assumed the guy was not feeling well or had left the island.

Wednesday's dive schedule featured more dives around Little Cayman Island. There were plenty of different dive sites along the reef and wall.

Carlos Hodges had a large bandage on his arm and stayed on the dive boat. When John asked him about his injury, Carlos had explained that he had snagged his arm on a nail in the dive locker room the day before. Carlos did not have the bandage during dinner, the night before. John thought it odd that Carlos would be in the dive locker room after dinner. Something was definitely strange about the Hodges.

They were nice enough, but John decided it was best to keep an eye on them.

On their first dive that morning, John and Rhonda took a big stride off the back of the dive boat and quickly dropped below the waves. They descended straight to the sandy bottom below. The first day they had to stop often after descending the first two feet to equalize the pressure in their ears. By this time clearing the pressure in their ears was second nature. John and Rhonda were the second diver pair off the boat. After there was a group of eight divers on the bottom near the mooring line, they all started swimming toward the reef heads. Their small group had gone several hundred yards from the boat when they heard a very clear voice say "All Holliday divers, return to the boat. All Holliday divers return to the boat." That was the name of another dive boat that had moored about eight hundred yards to the east of their dive boat. The divers in their group all swam towards each other and then joined up with a dive master and two others.

Suddenly there were two loud horn blasts from the underwater alarm equipment on their dive boat. In the safety briefing they had been instructed to stay down if they heard the alarm sound twice. This meant the dive boat was starting its engines. In a few seconds, from sixty feet below, they saw the hull of their dive boat race away.

They slowly surfaced and swam towards a mooring buoy a few hundred feet away. They stayed on the surface, and, after a few minutes, they saw the Holliday dive boat motoring towards them. This was not their dive boat. It had about eight divers and three crew on it. The Holliday boat crew indicated they should move away from the mooring ball. The boat temporarily tied itself to the mooring ball and then motioned for everyone to get on board. After everyone was on board, the captain informed them that there had been a medical emergency with one of the divers on their boat and their boat had taken the diver to shore.

When they got back to the dock, they learned that a man in their group named Javier had started his dive with a headache that turned out to be a migraine. This caused him to have vertigo when he got about fifteen feet below the water. His dive buddy recognized that he was in trouble and pulled him back to the surface. Out of caution the crew of the dive boat took him back to shore for medical evaluation. The guy named Javier turned out to be John's contact at the Grand Cayman airport. John didn't like the coincidence. Instead of leaving their dive equipment hanging down at the dock side drying room, John took their equipment back to their room and placed it in the shower to drip dry. He didn't want to chance anyone messing with their equipment during the night. They kept their dive equipment with them or in their room for the rest of the week.

Thursday morning, they were told on the dive boat that Javier, the injured diver, had been taken to the main island Grand Cayman, where there were better medical facilities. Thursday's evening dive included two brief encounters with reef sharks. The sharks decisively swam away from the divers and were never closer than fifty yards. John even chased one for a distance trying to get a good photo. But with a few flicks of the tail the sharks quickly swam out of sight.

Thursday evening, at dinner, they were informed that there had been a drowning and a guy had been found dead in the surf. The police were there from Grand Cayman Island and would be conducting an investigation and questioning everyone. The interview was superficial; "Where and when did you first meet him? Where and when did you last see him?" Who was he with?".

John had a suspicion that the gash on Carlos Hodges arm and the dead man were connected. But he didn't say anything to anyone about it. For the rest of their stay John kept an eye on the Hodges. He didn't exactly follow them around, but he sure took notice when he did see them. He even managed to get a few photos of the Hodges without them noticing. He'd add these and his suspicions to his field report when they got home.

Before they knew it, the week was over, and it was time to pack everything up for the trip back home. All week they had good food to eat, got to dive some spectacular dive sites, saw all kinds of marine life, and made some good friends with fellow divers. It was sad to leave this paradise where everything stopped and you quickly became one with the sea, the surf, and the sandy beaches.

The flight home was uneventful. They only unpacked what they needed and left everything else to be unpacked and put away the next day. It was so nice to be home in their own bed. After a long day of airports and flights, they went to bed early. The next day John took all the dive gear to the driveway and got a large tote, water hose, and air compressor ready. While they had dunked all their diving gear in fresh water on the dock in Little Cayman, it still needed to be cleaned and dried. The sun was bright and warm. The gear would dry quickly.

Tuesday morning John returned to work at the FBI's Little Rock Computer Lab. He had an email notification that he had a conference with Director McKenzie at nine that morning. By the time he waded through his emails, it was time to head to McKenzie's office. John suspected the meeting would be about his trip to Grand Cayman.

John knocked on McKenzie's door frame. McKenzie got up from his desk and motioned John to a small conference table.

"Yes, John, come in and please close the door. How was your trip?"

"It was very nice. Rhonda and I ALMOST had a great time SCUBA diving and just chilling."

"Do you have the memory stick?"

"Yes." John retrieved the memory stick from his shirt pocket and slid it towards McKenzie. McKenzie picked it up.

"I guess you heard about your contact?"

"Yes, a diving accident or something. They said his name was Javier. They ended up taking him to the hospital in Grand Cayman. We never heard exactly what happened."

"John it was no accident. It was expertly made to look like a diving related accident, but it was really an assassination. He died Saturday morning while you were flying home. The official cause of death was an un-diagnosed brain aneurysm. Almost unheard of in a thirty-two-year-old male in perfect health."

"Any more information on how or why he was killed?"

"Not at this time. He wasn't one of ours. He was an operative from a foreign government. So, we have to go through back channels to find out anything more."

"Do you think I was targeted as well?"

"It depends on if anyone saw you and the contact together at the Grand Cayman airport."

"What about the other dead guy?"

"We are checking on him. Haven't found anything yet. He was just a guy that liked to SCUBA dive a lot. But he didn't drown by accident. He had help. They found bruising on the neck consistent with strangulation. Looks like it happened sometime Wednesday night."

John thought about that for a minute. He had tossed the air tag in a trash bin at the Grand Cayman airport after getting the memory stick. He had been fairly observant of his surroundings when he was approached by the contact. No one else was in that part of the airport and he hadn't spotted any cameras.

"I don't think anyone observed us together."

"Even if they had made you at the airport. It would take some time for them to decide who you were and what to do about it. I would guess the drop was clean and no one spotted you. Why do you think the contact was on your dive boat?"

"I didn't like that coincidence. But unless they knew who I was before I got to Grand Cayman there is no way they could have pulled that off at the last minute. I asked the clerk at the Little Cayman Beach Resort about last-minute bookings. She said all the rooms had been reserved weeks before and there were no open rooms. As for the dive boat assignments, at check in they put friends and couples together on the same dive boats. But beyond that, it's first come first serve. Again, unless they knew who I was ahead of time, there is no way they could know which boat to request."

"I guess we will have to wait and see. Did you take a look at the memory stick?"

"No. I was supposed to be on vacation."

"The data is encrypted. I have the password and will forward the data to the operations group. Welcome home. Did they pay for your vacations to the Caribbean in the CIA?"

"No."

"Well, don't expect it to happen again here either. It was just a one-time deal. If anyone asks, tell them it was a negotiated, sign on bonus."

"One more thing. I may have photos of the assassins."

"Assassins? As in more than one?"

"Yes."

"What makes you think they are assassins?"

"Lots of little things. I might be wrong. But we definitely need to look into it. It'll all be in my field report tomorrow."

"Anything else?"

"Nope. Spies, encrypted info drops, assassins, murder, dead people. That's it. Oh, and just to be clear. This was nobody's idea of a good vacation, ever!"

"I look forward to seeing some pictures of those famous Little Cayman Island sunsets you told me about."

Chapter 18

~

The next week Jill Stephens called John into her office. She liked the way he had created custom queries to pull the data from the various databases.

"I heard you and the wife took a little Caribbean vacation last week."

"Yes mam. Little Cayman Island is a great place for SCUBA diving. Do you SCUBA dive?"

"No way. I'm a beach bum. I like to be near the beach."

"The white sandy beaches and sunsets are picture perfect there."

"I've got a question about that report you did before you left. From what you have seen of our computer facilities what do you think it would take to build an AI search engine to create the same type reports?"

"Not much really. Hardware wise, a few multiprocessor servers and a few drive arrays. The application development could take a while. I know most of the key modules and I've got a pretty good idea how the Artificial Intelligence modules should formulate the queries. The reporting piece is a pretty easy build. I would guess it might take six to nine months to develop the AI search engine. It would be better if we had someone with AI development experience on the team."

"Do you think this is something we can do in house?"

"If you can get someone with AI development expertise on board, we could definitely do this in house."

"Would you be willing to work with a contractor to build this for us? You'd be lead and the contractor would report to you."

"Sounds like a fun project. When do we start?"

"I'll have to run this up the ladder and see if we can get the funding approved. But this is something I think we need to develop to stay current. I'll let you know next week."

Thursday morning John had an intraoffice email informing them of a new email and document encryption standard for government use. It detailed when and under what circumstances the new encryption systems should be used. The email included links to download and install the encryption modules on government computer systems. John downloaded the program and installed it as instructed. After he was convinced, it was installed properly, he started locating the compiled code modules that had been installed on his office computer. He copied them to a separate directory and started running a program to decompile the modules. He recognized most of the code from the team he worked with at the CIA computer labs. He had helped build most of this code. But there were some extra subroutines he hadn't seen before. These interested him most of all. He studied them to figure out what they were doing. One was a formatting routine used for emails and another one of the new subroutines was for identifying various file types. But buried in the code, at the end of one of the new subroutines, there were several lines of code that made no sense. It took John a while to track the variables these lines of code used. They were set at various places throughout the code. Just a line or two of code here and there. It was a whole subroutine that had been dispersed throughout the entire module and in multiple subroutines, so it was difficult to follow. After a few hours John had traced all of the variables and code snippets. He copied them out and organized them with notes on how and when each was executed. It was a backdoor that decrypted any message encrypted with this system if the password entered was "Harpcrates". John did a google search for "Harpcrates". Apparently

"Harpcrates" was the name of the Greek god of secrets. This was a huge backdoor to the new government encryption system.

As was his custom, John took some time to himself. He needed to decide how to proceed. He left the FBI campus and went to Texas Roadhouse restaurant for lunch. The place was pretty busy at lunch. The hostess frowned when John turned down a seat at the bar. He asked for a booth instead. He needed to sit alone for a while and consider his options.

He had to make sure the backdoor got exposed and fixed. This could be a breach of national security. He had to assume whoever put that back door into the encryption system would kill to not have it discovered. The trick was not to become the target. John decided to punt that hot potato as far away as he possibly could. Could they already know he found the back door when he did that Google search for "Harpcrates"? Man, he needed to do whatever he was going to do fast. No telling if this back door was purposely put in by the government or an external entity.

He should tell his current boss, Jill Stephens and maybe McKenzie the director. But this encryption system was rolled out to all government branches. He thought of the CIA counterpart, McGuire operations director in Houston and Ms. Riley, the manager over at the CIA computer labs in Houston. Then there was Robert Sanders and the guys he met at Langley. Robert might be in on it as the code was created in his computer lab. It looked like a blast email was the way to go. Once the cat was out of the bag, there would be no reason to come for him he hoped.

John took a napkin and started making a list of all the email addresses he had for FBI, CIA, and whatever else branch of the government he could think of. In the end he had about a two-dozen email addresses that spanned the CIA, FBI, and State Department. They covered the State Department, CIA Operations, CIA Computer Lab, CIA Field Agents, FBI Director of Operations, FBI Computer

Labs, FBI Field Agents, Langley, plus a few administrative assistants thrown in for good measure. Basically, everyone John knew or had heard of in the government. He decided to look up a few senators and the National Security Administration (NSA) department email addresses to add to the email as well.

The email would be simple and straight to the point. The new encryption system rolled out that week in the FBI and presumably for all branches of the government had a back door that allowed anyone to read any email using the password "Harpcrates." This could be easily verified and checked by anyone who had installed the new mandated encryption system.

John used his phone to create the email while he sat at lunch. He would send the email to his office email at the FBI. When he was back at the office, he would cut and paste the email body into an email with all the email addresses. The subject line would read 'Massive Encryption Security Breach in new government encryption modules.

He would have preferred to send the email anonymously. But he decided it was better to be straight forward with such an urgent issue. He finished his lunch and headed back to the FBI offices. He felt better now that he had a direction and course of action.

When he got back to the computer lab, he was surprised to find his logon ID was somehow suspended. The IT security help line could not explain it and they could not unlock his FBI logon account. Someone knew he was wise to the back door. John thought for a moment then he remembered the servers in the lab used admin access to logon to the FBI network. He went into the computer lab and closed the door. The server was really just a high-performance computer with a huge hard disk array attached. John used the administrative password to open the terminal screen. He logged onto his personal web server and copied his fake email program to the server's local hard disk. He launched it and crafted the email. He added a line about his FBI logon being suspended after he did a search for "Harpcrates". Then He sent the email with his

FBI email address. He hoped that would be enough to get the backdoor shut down.

Friday John's FBI logon was mysteriously unsuspended. He found that several of the people had responded to his email about the back door.

Friday evening about thirty minutes after John got home, there was a knock on the door. There were two FBI field agents at his door. They identified themselves and informed him that they were there to protect him and his family. They would be watching the house for the next few days. John asked them why? Neither of them knew why. They were just assigned to the detail to watch the house. John thought he was no longer a threat to anyone. So why the security? John asked them if they could remain as inconspicuous as possible. It was a dead-end road and any cars on the street would stand out. They assured John that they would stay out of sight as much as possible.

Saturday about mid-morning, John heard another knock on their front door. It was yet another guy in a suit. His credentials said he was from the state department. Apparently, he was there to take John's statement about the diving accident at Little Cayman. John told him he didn't know the guy or speak to him prior to the dive. He told the agent that he and his wife were several hundred yards away and sixty feet below the diver when the emergency happened. The agent took John's statement and left.

At noon, Bryan, the neighbor across the street, had noticed all the traffic and texted John to ask if everything was OK. John assured Bryan that everything was fine and that it was just some guys trying to make sure he didn't need to shoot anyone. They both laughed.

John never knew exactly which email recipient got the NSA stirred up. But they were all over the encryption security breach. They interviewed John. He told them how he had helped to develop the basic encryption system up to a point. He told them how after he left the CIA team it was further developed, packaged, sent for approval, and finally rolled out. He told them how he discovered the encryption system's backdoor. He wasn't sure how much the agent that interviewed him understood. But he just told them how it had happened and hoped someone reading the report would understand it. This was going to be a witch hunt and one or more people would ultimately end-up in federal prison or much worse. It was scary to think that there are literally places that the government can send you that you will never be heard from again. But, while never seeing one in person, John was certain these types of places did, in fact, exist.

It was Wednesday, within a week of sending his email, when John received an interoffice email that contained links to an updated encryption program to fix unspecified bugs that had been discovered in the previous version of the encryption software. Well, that was progress. John would have to decompile some of the new modules and see if they had indeed removed the malicious code. That would have to wait till another day. Today John wanted to get started on the high-level architecture for the new FBI AI search engine. He started by mapping out the major functions, the inputs, and outputs. This was going to be a really fun project.

Two weeks later John and Rhonda were driving to Gulf Shores. They were going to enjoy the week visiting with Mike and Linda Lambert who lived in Foley. Mike had been John's mentor when he was brought on board with the CIA. Mike and John had been good friends ever since. Mike had helped John out of a few rough spots that resulted from the Prophet X program. Currently Mike was retired from the CIA and

John couldn't wait to see the change in Mike since his retirement. The pressures of the job he had at the CIA were oppressive. John suspected Mike would be different in a good way.

They would make the eight-hour drive to Gulf Shores today, check into their rental beach house late that evening. The next day John and Rhonda would have lunch at Mike and Linda's house in Foley.

Mike greeted them with his big broad grin and an equally big hug.

"How was the drive down from Arkansas?"

"Long! But the opportunity to hang with you high class types made the trip worth it."

They both laughed. After a few polite words Mike took John to the back patio where he was grilling some steaks.

John said, "Man those smell and look great!"

"They'll eat if I don't burn them. Hey, someone told me about an encryption back door you found. What's up with that?"

"Do you remember when I had to go to Langley and help their crypto guys package my encryption routines for government use?"

"I remember you making a pretty penny selling your encryption program. So, what about it?"

"You know me. If there's a fresh cow patty out there, I'll find a way to step in it."

"Ha, ha! Is that an Arkansas thing. I've never heard anyone say that before." Mike was laughing hard.

"After I helped them understand my encryption routines, we brainstormed for a few weeks and laid out the subroutines for a super-duper encryption program. That's about when I left Langley and came home. They were going to develop it for use in government communications. Anyways, about a month ago I'm working with the FBI in Arkansas when I get an email about a new standard email encryption system everyone is supposed to install. I got the impression it was rolled out in most all government branches. Naturally when I installed it, I studied the encryption program modules. It was mostly the stuff I had worked on with the crypto team in Langley. They had added some functions and things. But then I found some stuff that didn't make since and I started studying it. Long story short, I found a hidden back door that allowed anyone to circumvent the encryption."

"So, what did you do about it?"

"I sent out an email exposing the back door to everyone in the CIA, FBI, State Department, the Langley guys, and any senator I could think of. It didn't take long. Less than one week later there was a bug fix for the encryption program."

"John, let me tell you what I heard. There was someone in our own government somewhere that wanted a back door into your encryption system. They got leverage on one of those Langley guys and had him put the back door in. Then he was in a fatal accident. Not a coincidence. Anyway, there is a huge witch hunt right now. Preliminary investigation points to someone high up in the NSA. Speculation says, whoever it was, got paid off big time by and outside foreign entity."

"Do tell. Mike, that's exactly the kind of stuff I'm trying to stay away from."

"Wow! Now that I think about it. I'm not so sure Linda and I are safe with you here. You seem to be a trouble magnet. Any cow patties around here we need to know about?"

They laughed as Mike turned the steaks one last time.

"Rhonda and I just want to settle back down to a semi-normal life like we had before the Prophet X program. I'm starting to wonder if we will find that in Arkansas or not. Maybe I just need to learn to leave stuff alone."

"I'd say you are doing exactly what you should be doing. You do realize the wake you cut through the CIA, don't you?"

"What do you mean?"

"At first, when we discovered you were operating alone, we all thought you had some kind of superpower. But then, after we got to know you, we all realized what we saw in you, really was a superpower.

You live the values most field people used to have and still believe in. I'm talking about the intangibles like honesty, integrity, and most importantly an actual relationship with God. These are things we all had or wanted to have at one time. Dredging through the sewers of life you make compromises and eventually lose sight of those things. You reminded us of a life we once lived or aspired to live. We all envied you and wanted your superpower, God's favor."

"Listen, Mike. I'm not paying for the steaks on that grill, no matter how much you flatter me."

They both laughed.

"John. All I'm trying to say is you made a huge difference in many of the guys lives at the CIA and I'm sure the guys at the FBI see the same qualities in you that we did."

John was feeling a little uncomfortable talking about himself.

"So, how are things here in Foley?"

"We love it. We just fell in love with the place from day one. We have great neighbors and have joined a local Baptist church. We are active in many of the church activities. Other than Sunday and mid-week services, Linda does something with a women's group, and I go to a men's prayer breakfast every Tuesday morning. It's a great place to get to know some of the guys in the church. John, it's everything we hoped for. It's great for me, for Linda and for our girls. I guess I've finally found what you were talking about when you described your life before the Prophet X thing."

"With a line like that, you guys should be selling real estate or running for public office around here."

"Maybe."

After a fabulous dinner and dessert, they drove to the beach, parked, and went for a long walk down the shoreline. The girls were walking a few yards in front of the guys, just out of ear shot. Sunset on the beach is a special time. It begs for reflection and in return promises peace. John always thought of God's power and majesty when he walked along the powerful roar of the surf on the sandy beaches.

John really enjoyed spending time with Mike. They openly discussed their relationship with Jesus and how they tried to walk daily in obedience to Him. They were brothers in Christ each trying to draw closer to God. After a while they both stopped talking and turned inward. They enjoyed the rest of the walk in silence. John was thinking about Kevin Baxley, the young man with such an amazing command of scripture. John wanted to find some way to be around Kevin more. John loved reading and talking about the Bible.

Thursday morning John met Mike at the dock. They were going deep sea fishing. The gulf was relatively calm. It was going to be hot out on the water. The captain and owner of the boat was one of Mike's friends. They all split the cost of the fuel and bait. This trip was all about putting fish in the freezer. They were after Snapper, but other fish were welcome. They headed out to a few of the best spots and caught several nice size fish. After about an hour John hooked a big fish. The big fish ran as his line quickly spooled out. The captain started the boat and motored in the general direction the fish was running. Eventually John was able to reel the fish close to the surface. It was a large shark. It was way too big for John to bring onto the boat with the small tackle John was using. The captain shut down the engines and ran to retrieve the gaff hanging on the wall in the galley. He made it to the side of the boat with the gaff just as John brought the large fish to the surface. He expertly hooked the shark with the gaff and pulled it alongside. As soon as he got the fish close to the boat, he asked John to release the tension on the line. The captain then cut the line and released the shark. While the shark was a great catch. It was much too large for freezer meat. After six hours the large ice chests were full of Snapper and Grouper, with a few Wahoos. An extraordinary catch for one day. They headed back to shore. There was a lot of work to be done cleaning the fish and putting the meat in freezer bags.

After a few days of visiting with old friends and seeing their old neighborhood it was time to move on down the coast. John and Rhonda once again said their goodbyes to Gulf Shores. They headed about an hour east, towards the beaches in Florida. They had rented a beach house at Navarre Beach. It was their first visit to the area.

After they dropped off their luggage at the beach house, they went to find a good place to eat. Without knowing the area, it was difficult to decide on where to eat. They drove around to see what was in the area and finally stopped at a place called Scooter's Fish House. The food was great, and they got there just ahead of the dinner crowd.

The next morning, they got up early, loaded their SCUBA diving gear and headed to Destin. John had booked a SCUBA diving charter with Niuhi Dive Charters. They found the boat and got their gear out of the car. This was going to be a very special dive. The dive site was twenty-two miles off the coast. The Gulf could be quite rough out there. John had read where several people had complained that they drove to Destin only to have their dives on this site canceled due to rough water, strong currents, or poor visibility. But the Lord was good and it looked as if John and Rhonda would get to make the dive. The dive site was the aircraft carrier USS Oriskany. It is the world's largest manmade reef. The aircraft carrier sits upright, two hundred and twelve feet below the surface in the Gulf of Mexico. The top of the ship reaches up to within eighty-five feet of the surface. John and Rhonda would be diving down to maximum depth of one hundred and twenty feet, about twenty-six feet above the flight deck. This would be one of the deepest dives John or Rhonda had been on. John was wondering how bad the currents would be this far out in the Gulf of Mexico.

The morning air was already humid and breezy, as they carried their equipment to the boat dock. John had spotted the charter boat and they put their equipment on the dock near the boat. It is always a good idea to wait until asked to board a boat. Several other cars had arrived, they too were piling equipment on the boat dock. In a few minutes the captain and crew arrived and began loading SCUBA tanks on the boat. When they had most of the tanks onboard, they invited everyone to bring their gear onboard.

After the boat ride out to the site, everyone got ready for the dive. There were six divers, one master diver and the boat captain. Three of the other four divers were tech divers. They each wore double tanks on their backs and a side mounted tank. They would be diving into the structure below the flight deck and then to the sandy bottom at two-hundred and twelve feet. The fourth diver was diving a rebreather with two side mount tanks. He was going straight to the bottom and then riding the current as he spearfished for Lionfish. John and Rhonda followed the master diver down to the ship's super structure. They were going to be making a couple of spiraling circuits around and down the super structure. Then they would work their way back up the super structure and on to the dive boat.

At the top of the super structure two flags fluttered in a light current. One was an American flag and the other was a P.O.W. flag. As John looked down at the flags, he noticed the gray shape gliding just forty feet below them. It was a seven-foot bull shark. It was just cruising around the ship hull, looking for an easy snack. As they began the circuit down and around the ships super structure, the massive size of the aircraft carrier became apparent. The visibility was better than expected. There were all kinds of fish around the super structure. The ship was covered with coral growth, but still retained a lot of detail. John had brought his underwater camera on the dive, and he took many pictures.

Forty-five minutes later they were back on the dive boat, the other four divers started their dive. They would be down longer and ride the currents some distance from the Oriskany. After a planned surface interval to allow most of the excess nitrogen loading to dissipate from their bodies, John and Rhonda went down and made another circuit around the aircraft carrier's super structure. The size of this ship was amazing. You could dive here dozens of times and never see half of it. John saw a couple of more sharks on the second dive and near the top of the ship was a couple of barracudas. The barracudas were amazing to watch. They used their lightning-fast swimming speed and razor-sharp teeth to cut other fish in half. But mostly when they are on a dive site, they are stationary, just watching. They aren't the kind of fish to play with.

After they were back on the boat from their second dive, the captain untied from the mooring ball and started motoring east, with the currents. The other divers had surfaced about half a mile from the Oriskany dive site. The boat captain expertly cut the engines, drifted past the divers and threw them a rope. The guy on the rebreather would surface another quarter of a mile east. With everyone aboard and all equipment stowed, the boat started the twenty-two-mile trip back to shore.

They had booked two more SCUBA dives for the following day. These had been booked from a charter named Shark Quest. These would be dives in the relatively shallow waters around Destin. Their first dive on a shallow reef. It had very poor visibility and they could only see a few feet. After about twenty minutes they surfaced and got back in the boat. The captain asked them about the visibility. John said, "Maybe three feet or less. Not much to see." The captain recovered the other four divers and headed for what he hoped would be a better dive site. The visibility at this second site was about the same.

The captain motored about forty minutes away and dropped the divers on an old barge. The visibility here was good and they could see about seventy-five feet. After swimming around and inside the barge hull, John had Rhonda stay in the hull with the ribs as a background. He floated about eight feet above and just outside the hull. After taking the photo, John caught a glimpse of something big and dark moving in his peripheral vision. As he turned, he found himself within ten feet of a city bus sized whale shark. It was huge. It was effortlessly gliding by. Following it were two large manta rays. The rays had wing spans of seven to eight feet each. John was snapping photos as they slowly glided by. Everyone in the group was excited at this rare sight and talked about their experience on the boat ride back to shore.

The next morning, they began packing all their bags into the car. John phoned Don McCarthy.

"Hi John. What's up?"

"Rhonda and I are in Destin, Florida this morning. We're fixing to leave, and I wondered if you and Ms. Deloris might be free for dinner this evening?"

"As far as I know we don't have any plans. Are you guys headed this way?"

"We can be. If you guys are free for dinner."

"Sounds great. When will you be here?"

"We should be there around four this afternoon. I've never been to Kenner. You want us to drop by your place or meet somewhere?"

"I'll send you our address in a text. Do you have a place to stay? "

"I was going to get us a room at that La Quinta Inn on Williams Boulevard. Is that a good place to spend the night?"

"Yes. But you guys can stay here if you like. We have a spare bedroom."

"Thanks for the offer. But we will be heading out pretty early. I think we will just do the hotel for the night. See you around 4pm."

"OK. Be safe."

When Rhonda came back into the house, John told her, "Slight change of plans. I thought we might as well swing by and see Don McCarthy on our way home. I told him we would have dinner with them tonight. I hope you don't mind."

"Not at all. I would love to see Don and Deloris again. It's been years since we've seen Deloris."

Soon they were on the road to Kenner, Louisiana.

As they pulled up to the address Don had sent John, Don opened the front door and greeted them. John had made the hotel reservation shortly after leaving Destin that morning. After visiting for a few minutes Don suggested they might want to head to a restaurant.

"What are you guys hungry for?"

"Seafood of course."

Deloris said, "Kenner Seafood is the best around here. We can take our car."

"OK. It sounds like we're in your hands. Lead the way."

They drove just a few miles to the Kenner Seafood restaurant. After a relaxing dinner they went back to the McCarthy's house. The girls went into the kitchen to visit and make some coffee.

"John, what did the CIA have you doing?"

"Consulting mostly. But not about computer stuff. Seems like the government has a hard time thinking its way out of a paper bag without burning the whole thing down. There was this guy that seemed to like the solutions I came up with better than their scorched earth policy."

"What kind of problems?"

"Umm, like someone would be suspected of doing or stealing something and they needed to resolve the issue. They have a whole lot of nasty tricks that can pretty much ruin your life for a very long time. They tend to think in terms of their absolute power over a situation. I showed them there are easier ways to accomplish their goals, without burning down someone's house.".

"Burning down someone's house?"

"Not really, just ruining their world."

"You always did your best thinking outside the box."

"I always wondered, after I went away to Europe for a month, what exactly did they do to convince you to keep me on at the utility company?"

"It was a Saturday morning, in this living room. I will remember it for as long as I live. They sat down, two of them, men in suits and ties. They explained to me that certain troubles could befall people if the IRS got some bogus financial information. They indicated that certain higher ups in the utility company could suddenly be convinced that I was no longer needed. They discussed how easy it was to get the police thinking someone was somehow tied into drugs moving in and out of Louisiana. Then, they politely ask me to seriously consider finding a way to keep you employed by the utility company. I think it was something along those lines."

"Sorry, I've seen them do those things and worse."

"Na, they just gave me incentive to do what I wanted to do anyway. But I knew you were double dipping, working for them on the side. I thought it was programming stuff."

"Well, I did do a few programming projects for them. I helped them build an encryption system. I think they are deploying it nationwide for secure emailing."

"I didn't know you knew anything about data encryption."

"It was interesting, so I studied and built my own encryption program. The problem was the government couldn't read my encrypted messages and wanted my encryption program. So, I sold it to them. Did you know they have AI computer systems for breaking encryption and data searches?"

"No, but it figures. Did you get to play with the AI stuff?

"Yes, I put in a few days playing with their AI systems."

"So now what's the plan, now that you divorced the CIA and the utility company?

"Not sure. I'm working with a friend from high school. He's got me working at the local FBI offices computer lab. It's interesting work."

"Never a dull moment around you. I guess you're just attracted to that sort of excitement. "

"Not really, trouble just seems to find me."

They had coffee and visited until nearly midnight. Rhonda and John finally said their goodbyes and went to their hotel room.

On the long drive back to Arkansas John and Rhonda talked about all the friends they missed in Gulf Shores and Houston. Then John told Rhonda he was going to find a way to spend some time with Kevin Baxley. She knew John liked being around other Christian men and Kevin seemed to have a special connection with John.

Chapter 19

~

Tuesday morning the doorbell rang. John checked the camera feed from the front porch on his phone. It was Luke Morgan. John opened the door and invited Luke in.

"Man, I never would have guessed you'd be coming up here to back woods Arkansas to see me. Must be important."

"Back woods? Man, it's great to be out of the city and around all these beautiful trees."

"Yep, the landscape is definitely different here. I'm sorry. I believe you've met my wife Rhonda before."

"Yes Mam. Nice to see you again."

"Since when do they send computer geeks on house calls? My computers are running just fine, by the way."

"I'm not a computer tech anymore. I am a field asset now and I need to ask you something."

Sensing the urgency of Luke's visit John said, "Hon, could you get Luke and me a tall glass of iced tea?"

"Sure, Luke would you like lemon in your tea?"

"Yes mam, please."

After Rhonda left the den, "Well, I guess you'll get around to it sooner or later. What's up?"

"They asked me to come and see if you'd build us a custom computer program."

"Why would I want to do that?"

"They were hoping you might be a patriot and help us fight a terrorist organization."

"I'm pretty sure that the ship with my patriot card sailed away when you guys tried to steal the Prophet X program I wrote, and then you chased me and my family halfway around the world."

"John, that was a long time ago. There's been lots of water under the bridge since then. Look, they just need an encryption program with a hidden backdoor. That's it. We'll do the rest."

"Seems to me I heard about just that kind of program being pushed out to government offices a little while back. Go find that guy and let him be your patriot."

"He's dead."

"Another great reason for me to say 'NO.'"

"John, listen. We really need this ready to deliver in two weeks. We have to get it in the pipe ASAP. The two major drug cartels are being persuaded that their communications are not secure. If we time this right and can get them to use our encryption program, then we can read their whole network and take them down totally."

"So, if I do this, then the drug cartel will be hunting the guy that sent them the bogus encryption program. Which would be me and my family? Did anyone ever tell you that you really suck at trying to get someone to help you? Because you do! The more your mouth moves the more reasons I hear why NOT to do this."

"I'm just being honest with you."

"Yeah, well that's a new trick for the CIA. Honesty! Wow! What a concept."

Luke decided to just shut up and let John process for a minute or two.

Rhonda came back in with the iced tea. She could tell John was tense about something. So, she picked up the conversation. "So, Luke, is there someone special back in Houston?"

"No mam. The job keeps me pretty busy. There is a girl at the gym that I'm friends with. I've been thinking about asking her out."

"I'm sure she would be thrilled to know you are interested."

John was staring deep into his glass of ice tea. He was thinking. Building the encryption program would be easy. If he buried the back door in the code, like the one he had found in the government email program, then chances were no one would find it. He had found that back door because he had developed most of the routines to begin with. Still, if this came back on him, then the cartels would never quit looking for him and his family. The real problem was how to isolate himself from the code. There could be no way it would ever be traced back to him.

"Luke, there is something out back I want to show you."

Rhonda suspected something was going on and John didn't want her to hear.

"Luke, stay seated. John, I have a right to know what's going on. I'm not stupid. He didn't come all the way from Houston just to say 'hi.'"

John was caught off guard. Rhonda usually went along with his judgement. But she didn't want them to be sucked back into another situation where they were in danger again. John reasoned she was right.

"Rhonda, you know that data encryption program I wrote and sold to the government?"

"Yes."

"Well, they want me to build another one except this one has a secret way that allows people to read the encrypted files with a special password. They are going to give it to the drug cartel to use for encrypted messages. Then, the CIA can read all of the drug cartel's encrypted emails."

"So?"

"So, when the drug cartel discovers the encryption system is bogus, they are going to want to kill the person that wrote it. Luke here thinks I will just build them the program because I'm a patriot. So, Luke, the problem is not building the encryption program. The real problem is not being tied to the bogus encryption systems development. I have a few ideas on how that might be mitigated. But I need to know who is in the loop here and now. Luke, the first question is who knows you're here?"

Luke was processing the sudden shift of the situation. Finally, he said, "McGuire sent me. He briefed me in his office. No paperwork. His admin made the travel arrangements. But she doesn't know why."

"Do you have a cell phone?"

"Sure"

"Good, let me see it."

John phoned McGuire's private cell phone. McGuire picked up on the second ring.

"McGuire, this is John Davidson. Luke here asked me to do something that would seem to be a quick way to get dead. Two questions. First, who suggested getting me to write the program?"

"No one. I ask Luke to speak to you."

"Second question, who's idea is it to give the cartel a bogus encryption system?"

"It's not a sanctioned operation. No teams, no reporting, no oversite. I want to implant the capability to read their mail before we do anything. Then, in a few months, we will assign an analyst to assess the value of the backdoor. Later, if there is enough data in their emails to make a significant impact, then we will put together a team."

"That sounds like a super great plan. But WHO GAVE YOU THIS IDEA?"

"It is my idea. You and Luke are the only ones I have mentioned it to."

"So, if my name pops-up in a report, or either of you tells anyone I was involved, or someone just figures out I likely wrote it, then what do you think will happen?"

"John, I see your point. But, listen."

John cut him off.

"Point is, if everything goes to your plan, then the cartel is going to want to kill whoever wrote the bogus encryption program and his whole family. That's the cartel way. McGuire, if you go down this path, then I guarantee people are going to die. McGuire, COUNT ME

OUT! I'm not ever working for you guys again. You think I'm stupid enough to put my family in danger, looking over our shoulders forever, just to help you out. And for what? Out of the goodness of my heart. Fat chance, fat man. Count this hillbilly out for good. LEAVE US ALONE!" John hung up the phone and tossed it back to a now pale-faced Luke. No one ever talked to McGuire like that and lived to talk about it. Rhonda knew bad things happen to people who push John and he seemed unusually upset at the moment. John watched the expressions on Rhonda and Luke's faces for a moment. The urge to grin was too great.

"Luke, buddy, do you think I might have set your career back just a little bit with that phone call?"

Luke was not amused, but very confused.

"Luke, when you get back to Houston, McGuire is going to want to take you to lunch." Luke was stupefied.

"Why, to fire me?"

"No, to see what it was that made me so mad. But he may need to reprimand you to pull this off. When he takes you to lunch, tell him we will need that Russian hacker that broke some of the bible codes. His name is in one of the old Prophet X operational reports. He'll know what I mean. I think I heard he is still working with one of the groups that extorts businesses with ransomware. Anyway, if we play our cards right, he's the guy that's going to develop the bogus encryption program and sell it to the cartel."

Luke was stunned. He was keeping up, but just barely.

"Luke, there is a security leak somewhere in the CIA. It's the same folks that recently arranged the back door in the government encryption program. To pull this off McGuire is going to have to blacklist me in the CIA. He's going to have to tell everyone I'm no longer the CIA's friend. You alone will have to be the one to feed the encryption program to that Russian hacker and tell him where he can sell it. I can help you with how that might work if you and McGuire can't figure out how to handle it. You, McGuire, and me, no one else can be in on this. If you need some help let me know. I have a few resources that can make things happen. You're first assignment is to quietly find that Russian hacker. After he sells the bogus encryption program to the cartel, he needs to be quietly dropped into a prison somewhere, off grid. Later, when McGuire wants to use the data from the cartel's messages, he needs to stick with the story that the NSA has been instrumental in helping them obtain the information on the cartel."

Luke was wondering who was really running this operation. John seemed to be calling all of the shots.

"Luke, one more thing, you'll need to stay for lunch. I need to make a few adjustments to a little program. You'll need to take it with you. It will allow you and I to securely communicate."

"John, isn't sending encrypted messages what got you in trouble with the NSA a while back?"

"I've figured out a way around the Echelon's intercepts, I think. Don't worry, there's a good chance it will work."

Rhonda couldn't believe her ears. It sounded like John was putting them right back in a big mess. She had heard enough.

"John! You're not seriously going to put us through this again! You said we're going to settle down, live the quiet life, and be normal. Remember?"

"Rhonda, I promise. There is no way we are going to get drawn into this mess. Luke, tell McGuire that you'll need to make a few trips to Langley Airforce Base. I need you to meet with a guy named Robert Saunders. He's NSA director over their computer labs. Take him to lunch, ask him some questions about me, it doesn't matter. Just don't keep it a secret that you're going to Langley Airforce Base and meeting with Robert Saunders. You don't have to tell people why, just make two or three trips in the next few weeks. It will look like the NSA computer labs wrote the bogus encryption program, if this goes sideways. I will use the code that they rolled out with a back door as a pattern for the bogus encryption program we give the cartel. A close dissection of the bogus encryption program will reveal it must have come from the same programmer who built the last encryption back door that I found."

John paused to assess Luke's face.

"Luke, buddy blink twice if you're keeping up. Are you following me?"

Rhonda suppressed a giggle.

"Barely. When did you and McGuire dream up this plan?"

"Oh, McGuire doesn't know anything about it, yet. You're going to lay it all out for him at that lunch."

"He doesn't know? OK, then exactly how and when did you dream up this plan?"

"Dude, I'm just makin' this stuff up as I go. You actually thought I had a plan? Really?"

John was grinning. Luke had forgotten how creative John was. He remembered hearing someone once say that John not only lived outside the box he excelled there. This seemed to be one of those acceleration points for John.

"Rhonda, I promise this thing is never, ever, coming back on us. I write the program give it to these guys and were done. Trust me, we will be safe. Are things sounding a little better, I hope?"

"John, it sounds complicated."

"That's the general idea. Blow some smoke in their eyes and toss them a few bones."

John could tell she still wasn't happy about it. But, he had most of the major pieces mapped out and she could tell he was committed at this point.

"Look, I need to do some programming stuff for an hour or so, then we can eat lunch. That will give us all a little more time to consider how to proceed. Luke, why don't you stay here and watch the TV while Rhonda prepares our lunch."

"Sounds good. I think."

John went to his home office and started making adjustments to the new encryption scheme he had been working on. It was not based on email at all. It used an FTP service that was still running on an old Linux server. Eons ago it was used as a Bulletin Board server. Why it was still online was a mystery. John still had access via a bogus account he had set up 20 years ago. The program he was writing added a random paragraph or two to the start of the encrypted message file. As it was decrypted this paragraph was removed. This added paragraph was converted from English to Klingon (a Star Trek fictitious language) before being added. The thought was that if the file transfer was captured by Echelon, then it would automatically be misfiled as a foreign language rather than an encrypted message. The encryption itself was just a re-arranged version of the encryption routines he had given to the N.S.A. When a message was copied from the server, it was automatically deleted on the server. After about an hour John had the program ready to go and loaded it on a small memory stick.

Rhonda had prepared some leftover pork chops, green beans, mashed potatoes, and dinner rolls for lunch. The smell of savory aromas were filling the house by the time she had lunch ready. Luke didn't get many home-cooked meals, and this was a real treat.

As they were eating John told Luke to use code names for communications. They would also use the name "Russel Hackman" instead of "Russian hacker" in communications. Similarly, "McGuire" would be "Big Mac". There were half a dozen cryptic words that they would use to confuse anyone able to unencrypt the messages. They also agreed to never use each other's name in any messages. John reminded Luke about checking his computers for spyware or key loggers. Luke was well aware of these computer security precautions.

"John, I have a question. Why. Why write this bogus encryption program for us?"

"You gave me several good reasons not to write the program. So, now I'll give you one reason why I should. Because my friend McGuire asked me to. He wouldn't ask unless he needed it. That being said, I love solving problems and I think we can solve this one without getting me killed."

They had finished lunch and Rhonda was putting away dishes.

"Luke are you familiar with the word 'reciprocity'?

"No."

"It is spelled R-E-C-I-P-R-O-C-I-T-Y. It is defined as the exchange of things with others for mutual benefit."

John retrieved a scrap of paper and a pen from the side table and slid it across the coffee table to Luke. Please write reciprocity in lower case on the paper."

Luke did as requested.

"Now in front of the word 'reciprocity", in caps write 'FRM2Y' and following 'reciprocity write in caps 'FRY2M.'" John looked at the paper.

"Good, this is the password we will use for the communications tool I built for us. The 'FR' stands for 'FROM', the 'M' stands for 'ME', the 'Y' stands for "YOU' and the number 2 stands for the word 'TO.'"

"The password is 'FRom Me 2 You reciprocity FRom You 2 Me' right?"

"Please read the password to me."

Luke read the password out loud.

John turned the scrap of paper over. "Now please write the password again."

Luke did as instructed.

"Good." John took the paper and shoved it in his pocket. "Great thing about living out in the country, you can burn a little trash every now and then and no one cares. Here is a small thumb drive. It has the communication tool on it you and I, and only you and I will use. Don't give this to anyone else, not even McGuire. If he asks, tell him I gave you a special tin can with a very long string that only you can use. That's how us hillbillies roll up here in backwoods Arkansas."

Luke wanted to laugh, but he was sort of afraid too.

"Are you sure you have the password memorized?"

"FRM2YreciprocityFRY2M"

"Perfect! Luke, there is just one more thing. Don't ever come back here and don't call or contact us in any way. Use the communications tool I built for all contact from here on out. Your being here puts us at risk. Especially after McGuire blackballs me. And now I'm thinking, if you leave now, then you might still catch a flight back to Houston this afternoon."

"John, I drove from Houston. McGuire didn't want my destination broadcasted to accounting."

"Smart move. He might not be just another dumb bureaucrat after all. Would you like to spend the night here and head back to Houston in the morning? We have a spare bedroom."

"No, if I leave now, then I should get home before ten o'clock. I need to be back in the office tomorrow for a meeting. But thanks for the offer."

With that Luke thanked them again for lunch and backed out of the driveway.

Chapter 20

~

After such a big lunch, Rhonda thought a nice salad would be more than they needed for dinner. John had been in his study/office for the last three hours. She knew he was focused intently on the project. She had seen him consumed with projects before. It was best to just let him work until the project was finished.

She started cutting up the onion and bell pepper for the salad. She would put these in the fridge for now. Next, she would fry up a small chicken breast to dice up on top of the salad. The last piece of the meal to prepare ahead of time was the croutons. She took a few pieces of light bread, buttered, and seasoned them with garlic and Italian seasoning before cutting them into croutons. These would be well toasted in the air fryer and set aside for dinner.

Around 5pm John emerged from his study, and they began making the salads. They boiled some eggs, cut up some lettuce and tossed everything in a large mixing bowl. They added some shredded cheese and black pepper. After adding some thousand island salad dressing, they mixed it all up and put it in their salad bowls.

At the dinner table Rhonda asked, "How's the project going?" She was hoping John would keep her in the loop.

"I'm still working out a few things. The plan I laid out for Luke can be improved. If he and McGuire do their part, we have nothing to worry about. But I can still take some precautions to insure we stay safe."

"So, you think we are in danger again, already?"

"No, no. And I plan to keep it that way. But you know me. I cover all the bases. Even though I don't see how it could ever happen, I will assume somehow, someone will eventually connect me to the bogus encryption program. I will be ready for that if it ever happens."

"Can we trust Luke and McGuire?"

"Yes, but I also trust that the cartel has unlimited resources. So, I'll be prepared and plan a way out for us."

"Doesn't sound like we're going to be staying here very long."

"Don't worry. God has brought us this far. He will protect us. You'll see."

They ate their salads in silence.

Wednesday morning Luke got word that McGuire wanted to see him. He phoned and found that McGuire was in the office all morning with no meeting scheduled. As he walked into McGuire's office, McGuire didn't get up. He just said, "Shut the door, this isn't going to take long. I suspect John turned us down?"

"Yes and No"

"What does that mean, exactly?"

"He's a.... well, he says, he, he's got a plan."

McGuire stared at Luke for a long moment. Without looking, he pressed the intercom button on his phone.

"Yes, sir." Nancy replied.

"Do I have anything scheduled between now and 1pm?"

"No, sir. Good, I'm going to lunch early. I'll check back with you this afternoon."

"Luke, do you like burritos?"

"Yes, sir?"

"There is a Freebirds restaurant over on Taylor Street. It's a little bit of a drive, but man, I love their burritos. I'll meet you there at 11:00. We should be able to snag a table and talk."

Luke and McGuire sat and ate lunch at Freebirds and Luke told him John's plan.

McGuire let Luke do most of the talking as he ate his burrito. McGuire finally said, "Luke, he's right. I'm going to have to reprimand you and suspend your active status in field ops. It's the only way to get you off teams and free to take care of the Russian hacker. But, if you'll stick it out, I'll make it up to you down the road."

"What are you going to reprimand me for? Being John Davidson's friend?"

"I can make that work."

Luke did not like where this was headed at all.

"McGuire, how are we going to get the Russian hacker to sell the bogus encryption program to the cartel?"

"Easy, we let him steal it. Then, we tell the cartel where they can get it. Once I suspend you from active field duty, you can use the Prophet X field reports to find that Russian hacker. If John says he's in those reports, then that's where you'll start. You can have the computer geeks do their magic AI search and find where he's living. When they ask for the project charge code, tell them you are just following up on a hunch. Take them a box of donuts. Bribery still works. I have a friend over in Russia who is retired. He still owes me a favor. He's very good. He's sort of like a Russian version of John Davidson. Anyway, he'll get the Russian hacker to take the bait. Then, he will send one of the cartel bosses an anonymous gift - the name and address of the hacker that stole the encryption program. The cartel will buy, or more likely just take, the bogus encryption program from the hacker. Then we're in business. See, easy as pie."

"Sir, I've never made pie."

McGuire laughed. "Son, there is a first time for everything. Don't worry, it'll all come together."

John had been working on the bogus encryption program for a few days. He needed to step away for a bit. Since the shooting on their street, he had been concerned that Bryan might be struggling with coming to terms with killing someone, just as he himself was. He phoned Bryan and asked if they could go get some coffee. John pulled across the street and picked Bryan up. They went to the East End Café.

John asked Bryan, "Have you thought much about the shooting?"

"I did for a day or so. Then I realized they were going to kill someone if we didn't do something to stop them. Strange how the sheriff let us keep our guns. I thought they always took the weapons in for evidence."

"Yep, I agree, strange. I keep thinking there should have been a better way to solve the problem."

"With those guys, there was only one way to protect the Winstons."

"Perhaps. I just feel like I failed because I couldn't come up with a better solution."

"Look, when I was in the Rangers, they drilled in to us that we were the hammers, not the nails. That means when we are called, there are nails to be driven. And sometimes it's coffin nails. We were taught to accept that we might be called on to kill people. After a while you sort of get used to the idea. You hope that day never comes. But sometimes, there is only one path laid out before you. There's no other choice but to go forward."

John finally asked, "Did you ever shoot anyone before?"

"No. My unit was never deployed to an active war zone. I was stationed in Germany for a while. How about you? You ever shot anyone before?"

"Yes." There was a long silence as they sipped their coffee.

"A guy was shooting at Rhonda as she pulled out of our garage. I used that same 243 rifle to stop him."

Bryan wanted details. But he could tell it was a difficult memory for John.

John abruptly changed the topic. "So, how's everything going at your house? The girls treating you good?"

"We're doing fine. How about your place? Everything smooth sailing?"

"Well, I have a project I'm working on. It's a government thing. I don't have a lot of time to get it done. I'm just taking a little break. Soon as I get back to the house, I'll have to get back on it. If it works, it might help save some lives down the road."

"Sounds exciting."

"Not really. It's just boring computer programming stuff. It's challenging, but mostly just a lot of long hours of keyboard work. I guess I probably need to get back to it and I'm sure you have a full day as well."

They finished their coffee and went back home.

When John got back to his office, he checked the communications system he had setup with Luke. Luke had left a message.

Had a Big Mac for lunch. The teacher reprimanded a student yesterday. We have plans to see Russel Hackman perform. I will let you know when we have tickets. Your friend, Luke Skywalker

John grinned. The name '*Luke Skywalker*' was a character from the Star Wars movies. Luke Morgan did have some skills after all. John made a mental note not to underestimate Luke's capabilities again. John fired a message back to Luke.

Glad to hear the Big Mac went down well. I warned the student he would be reprimanded when he got home. I've been working on a new project. Should be ready for production next week. Hope you get the Russel Hackman tickets soon. If not, there are other shows in town. Your friend, John McClane

John sent the message. He used the name '*John McClane*' from a movie called '*Die Hard*' to sign the messages he sent to Luke. It sounded like McGuire was on board, Luke had been reprimanded and they had a plan to get the Russian hacker to pass the bogus encryption program to the cartel. So far, the plan seemed to be working. If they couldn't locate the Russian hacker, then they could just find some other low-life hacker instead. There were a lot of hackers in the world. But first, John had to finish his part.

John had the new encryption program up and running. There were enough changes in the way it encrypted data to make it very difficult for someone to break it. Now to build the back door. John had studied the back door in the encryption system the government had rolled out. He picked up some good ideas and thought of a few ways to better hide the back door. There were going to be some long hours involved in hiding this back door.

As much as he liked Luke and McGuire, John had to consider that either one of them could easily get him killed. Perhaps it would be prudent to remind them that they too had some skin in this game. John sent another message.

As usual, I have documented the development of this new product. You never know when documentation will be useful in formulating future solutions. Your friend, John McClane

Luke and McGuire would definitely understand that if the cartel came for John, then their names would be on the cartel's list as well.

John needed some time away from the project. He was working about 14 hours a day on nothing but the program. Staying focused for such long periods was sucking his brain dry. The old headaches were starting to return. Thankfully, the program was almost finished.

Sunday morning John and Rhonda went to church. John saw Kevin Baxley and his wife sitting across the way. He leaned over to Rhonda. "Can we invite the Baxley's over for dinner some night?"

"Sure."

John slipped out of his seat a walked over to Kevin. "Good morning."

"Yes, it is. How's it going John?"

"Great! Are you guys going to life group?"

"Well, we have visited a few."

"Dude, you guys need to come with Rhonda and me. Our class is called 'Truth Seekers'. You guys would fit right in, and we have a lot of interesting discussions in our class. What do say? Can you stick around and go to life group with us?"

"Sure, we'd love to."

"Great! After class maybe we can all eat lunch together. See you after the service."

John went back to his seat.

He told Rhonda, "We might get to have lunch with the Baxley's after class."

After the Life Group class, they went back to the Davidson's house for lunch. Rhonda had put on a pot roast that morning and all they needed was to pick up some dinner rolls.

Lunch was a great success. They discussed their families, the places they grew up, and places they had worked. Just getting to know each other. Kevin's parents had raised him attending church. Kevin's mother played the organ at their local church and before Kevin could walk, he was in church, listening to the preaching and teaching from the Bible.

After dinner John and Kevin went out on the back porch. John was showing Kevin his pellet gun. They were shooting some targets near the back fence, about 50 yards. The modified pellet gun pushed the small .177 caliber air rifle pellet at 900 feet per second. John used the pellet gun to deter the squirrels from tearing up the bird feeders. The slow or hardheaded rodents were buried, the smart ones stayed off the bird feeders and were routinely chased away by the Davidson's small dog, Sassy.

Sassy was a seven-year-old, short haired fox terrier. She was an inside dog that weighed all of six pounds. She was trim and lightning fast, clearing the four steps off the back porch in a single jump before racing to the back fence. Starting from thirty feet behind, she sometimes rolled a squirrel before it made it to the safety of the back fence, fifty feet away. The squirrels always recovered and jumped to the fence before Sassy was on her feet again. But then she would strut around the yard for a few minutes before returning to the back door, victorious.

"John, seems I heard something about you doing some shooting around here a while back."

"Yes, it was a very bad day."

"The way I heard it, you saved some folks."

"I don't know. It was just a really bad day. I had a problem to solve and I'm not so sure I chose the right solution."

"So, you had options?"

"Well, I suppose not. I guess I only had one choice at the time. I could shoot or let my neighbors be shot."

"I heard they had machine guns."

"I think there were a couple of full auto guns. They were spraying lead like they had tons of bullets. It all happened really fast once it started. Hey, see if you can hit that green target to the right."

Kevin fired and appeared to miss the target. "Just as I thought. I shoot funny and the guns set up for me. Try aiming a little lower. I think I have it shooting a little high at 50 yards."

"Why would you have it sighted in high at 50 yards?"

"Habit, I guess. I always set my rifles up for their maximum effective range. I'm not even sure what that would be for this little pellet gun. Hey, see that big tree in the middle, out in the field?"

"Yes."

"I popped a crow that was on a limb about halfway up that tree, from here. I figured it was about eighty yards. He fell and did a cripple chicken dance. His buddies were squawking up a storm. He hopped through the field a ways, and then he just flew off with all his buddies. I don't figure I hurt him much. But I was proud of the shot. I held about nine inches over his head when I shot. Man, I couldn't believe it when he fell."

"Wow, have you had a lot of practice shooting guns?"

"Sort of. I've been deer hunting from an early age. It was something my dad and I did every year. I used to go practice with the rifle every few weeks during the summer. I got my deer hunting rifle dialed in at 200 yards and worked out from there."

"What type of rifle did you deer hunt with?"

"Most always my Remmington 243 shooting factory loads. Remmington Core Lock 100 grain bullets usually. I grew up hunting on a timber company road. I covered about half a mile stretch of that road. At one time, anything within 400 yards was mine. When I was yong, I crippled a deer with a 30-30 and had to go find it. It was about the second time I had ever pulled the trigger on a rifle. I aimed about a foot high, at 125 yards. After that, I made it a point to be familiar with the ballistics of my gun and my limitations as a shooter."

"400 yards?"

"425 yards is my personal best. You ever do any hunting?"

"Sure, but 150 yards is about the longest shot I've ever had and that was hunting with a friend under a power line. But I missed the deer. I'm better with a brush gun, like your 30-30 or a shotgun, in the woods."

They talked about hunting for a while and occasionally shot the pellet rifle.

Eventually they said their goodbyes and the Baxley's were gone.

Rhonda and Pam Baxley enjoyed visiting and getting to know each other. They exchanged recipes and talked about their children, hobbies, and careers. They found that they both enjoyed quilting. Rhonda showed her a few quilts she had made.

That night as they cleaned the kitchen and dinner dishes, John and Rhonda talked about how they had enjoyed getting to know the Baxley's.

John started working on the bogus email program Sunday night. He only had a few hours of sleep and a few small meals when he finished developing the bogus encryption program Tuesday evening. He took a long hot shower and fell into bed. He slept for 12 hours. It was late Wednesday morning when he awoke. He had a cup of coffee and told Rhonda he had finished the program.

"So, what happens now?"

"I find out if Luke has his part done. If he does, then we will take a road trip to visit with Don and Debbie McCarthy. I'll drop off the program somewhere and they can come pick it up. Then, were out of it."

"Are you sure?"

"I've done what was right to do and I covered all our bases, as best I could. It's in God's hands now. We've always been in His hands. He will protect us."

"I know. But we seem to keep getting into these situations."

"I guess God gave you a looser when you met me."

"Don't ever say that. You are the best gift, other than salvation, that God has given to me."

They kissed and just held each other for the next few minutes."

Chapter 21

John sent Luke a message.

The new product is ready for marketing. Did we get the tickets for the Russel Hackman show? Your friend, John McClane

It had been almost a week since their last communication. When he checked for messages Wednesday afternoon John had a reply.

The Russel Hackman tickets have been secured and awaiting your arrival. Can you send us your itinerary? Your friend, Luke Skywalker

So, they were ready for the program. John copied the bogus encryption program to a small memory stick. He had to name the executable file something. He named the file 'imperceivable.exe'. It sounded legit. It would allow totally secure message encryption. Once a message was encrypted with this software only the password used to encrypt the message would decrypt it into readable text again. It was ultra-secure unless you had the password or knew the back door password.

John needed a place for the drop. It had to be somewhere between their house and Don McCarthy's place in Kenner, Louisiana. He decided to pick a spot in route for the drop. It was called a dead drop. John would leave the memory stick somewhere and then, later, tell Luke and McGuire where to pick it up. He looked at a map. His eye was drawn to Vicksburg, Mississippi. It was where I20 crossed their shortest route to Kenner, Louisiana. He'd find a place there to drop the memory stick with the 'imperceivable.exe' file on it. John phoned Don McCarthy.

"Hey, Don. This is John Davidson. How's life treating you?"

"Hello John. We're doing great. What's up?"

"Well, I thought Rhonda and I might come visit you tomorrow. Are you guys free for dinner? We're just dying to go back to the Kenner Seafood restaurant. But this time it's our turn to buy your dinner."

"Well, let me check with Delores and see what we have planned for tomorrow night. Hold on a sec."

John waited a minute or so.

"We're available. When will you be here?"

"Umm, around three or four tomorrow evening."

"Sounds great. We'll see you then."

"OK. Goodbye"

John might have to explain the sudden visit to Don. But it couldn't wait. The sooner this was done the better.

John told Rhonda they needed to leave for Don's the following morning. She understood the urgency of the trip and started packing. John made reservations at the La Quinta Inn on Williams Boulevard in Kenner, Louisiana. Rhonda phoned the Hendersons, across the street. They had a daughter that kept Sassy when John and Rhonda were out of town. However, she was staying at a friend's house, studying for semester exams. So, they decided to take Sassy with them. Sassy usually traveled well.

The next morning, they had coffee and left the house around seven. They took Sassy with them. It was almost eleven when they got to Vicksburg, Mississippi. John said, "Let's find someplace to eat."

He took the first exit after they crossed over interstate 20. He had looked the area over on google maps and found what he thought was an ideal place for the dead drop. They parked in the shade of some trees in the parking lot and opened the door windows, about one inch. Sassy would be fine. It was about eighty degrees, with a light breeze, and they were parked in the shade. John and Rhonda walked into McAlister's Deli for lunch. They were well ahead of the lunch crowd. They ordered their meal. John paid with cash to avoid leaving any electronic trail on their credit cards. Then they sat at a booth while their sandwiches were being made. John told Rhonda he'd be right back and made his way to the men's restroom. As he washed his hands, he made sure no one else was in the restroom. From his pocket he retrieved a memory card and a small pencil nub which had a length of gorilla tape wrapped around it. He handled the tape roll with great care. He made sure not to leave any prints on the device or tape as he taped the memory card to the back side and underneath the righthand sink. The gorilla tape would securely hold the memory card in place until it was retrieved. He took a paper towel and wiped the surface clean and attached the gorilla tape with the memory card under it. He used the paper towel to wipe and pressed the gorilla tape again once it was in place. The whole process took less than two minutes. He tossed the paper towels and pencil nub into the trash bin and went back to their table.

After lunch John put Sassy on her leash and took her out of the car. He got the water bowl out and gave her a drink. There was a freshly mowed grassy lot behind McAlister's Deli. Sassy needed and enjoyed the walk, relieving herself as needed. After a ten-minute walk, they were back on the road, headed to Kenner, Louisiana.

They had a great dinner with Don and Delores McCarthy at the Kenner Seafood restaurant. While saying their goodbyes, John handed Don an envelope. He simply said, "Read it when you get home." The next morning, they drove back home. John had taken enough cash to cover the hotel and all the gas and food for this trip. There would be no credit card trail to follow, and they left their phones in Arkansas.

Don opened the envelope. It contained a letter and a small USB memory stick.

Don, Thanks for having dinner with us. I have been working on a new communications program and thought we might use it. It should be a very secure messaging system. It only does text messages, at the moment. But I might expand it to send other types of files if I find it useful. The USB memory stick has a communications program on it. Use the password FRM2YcolleagueFRY2M to encode our messages.

Please use it to send me a message or two when you can. And please destroy this letter after memorizing the password. Thanks John Davidson

Don took the USB device to his laptop and ran the program file. A screen came up with a prompt that read:

'Press **S** to send a message, **R** to receive a message, or **X** to exit this program'. Don pressed 'S'. Another prompt came up 'Type your message'. Don typed a short message thanking John for coming down to Kenner to visit with them and clicked on the send button at the bottom of the screen. The screen cleared and a new prompt appeared, 'Please enter the password'. Don typed FRM2YcolleagueFRY2M and hit the enter key. A small progress bar appeared. In about three seconds the progress bar was replaced with 'Message sent.' And the original prompt: 'Press **S** to send a message, **R** to receive a message, or **X** to exit this program'. Don exited the program and shut down his laptop. He'd deal with the letter tomorrow.

John had developed the communications program with some safeguards in it. First the program everyone had was just a loader program. It downloaded the user interface into memory from an FTP server. Then the program changed the downloaded file name and location of the executable after every use. The program on the flash drive could not retrieve any messages until John added the user's computer credentials to a list. Retrieved messages were automatically deleted from the server. Once the computer credentials were verified then the program used a secure VPN channel to pass the message and password to the encryption part of the program which ran on another remote file server. Because the real program was on a server, John could make changes and upgrade it as needed. The loader program, the user interface and the encryption were all separated. John wanted to use it as is for about six months or so. When the immediate use for the program was long passed, he would run the real test on it. He would purposely use some trigger words to see if Echelon was reading his messages. But that could get him in trouble. He'd have to give that one a lot of thought before deciding to do it.

John sent the following message to Luke via the communications tool:

The McAlister's Deli, just south of I20 in Vicksburg, Mississippi says your order is ready, but the sink in their bathroom has a leak. Let me know how you like the takeout from there. Your Friend, John McClane

That should be enough to get them the program. John had done the best he could. He hoped, with God's help, it would be more than sufficient.

Luke got John's message. Saturday morning, he left Houston around five in the morning. He arrived at the Vicksburg McAlister's Deli a little after eleven. He retrieved the memory card from under the sink, ate a sandwich and drove back to Houston. That evening he sent John a message.

McAlister's sandwich was good. Looking forward to seeing Russel Hackman next week. Your Friend, Luke Skywalker

John sent a message back to Luke:

I saw some graffiti in the bathroom that read '4M2Cobsqure4U2C'. Is that some kind of gang thing? Your Friend, John McClane

They had the back door password. John's part was done.

Luke had located the Russian hacker named Dmitry. McGuire used his back channels to reach out to his old Russian friend Mikhail.

Three days after Luke's visit to Vicksburg, Mikhail had the chip, and was setting the trap for Dmitry to think he stole it. A little money here and there and the trap was set. Dmitry hacked a server a friend told him about and downloaded some programming files. He had been told these were expensive programs which he could sell on the black market. About that time a mid-level cartel boss was arrested and placed in a cell with a young hacker dude who talked about some super encryption program his buddy had stolen. Later, they all got out on bail. The Cartel eventually found Dmitry. Dmitry was seeing dollar signs when someone came to buy the program files he had stolen. But shortly after their first meeting, Dmitry was dead, and his computers were stolen.

It took a few weeks, but the cartel's use of the program was spreading. The Echelon group soon had a ton of encrypted texts for the NSA to look at. After several weeks, McGuire reached out to invite a friend in the NSA out to lunch. His NSA friend mentioned the proliferation of the new encrypted data that they were receiving. McGuire told him they had found an encryption program and password on a computer they had confiscated from a drug dealer. He offered to turn them over to the NSA as the CIA had no use for them.

Chapter 22

~

It took the NSA a few weeks to put it all together, the encrypted messages, the encryption program from the CIA and the back door password. But when they did all of the encrypted messages they had gotten from Echelon over the past two months were instantly decipherable. After the messages were analyzed, a joint task force with the NSA, CIA, and FBI was formed. Early on, the decision was made to use the information to gather as much information as possible about the leadership of the three major drug cartels. After their operations were shut down, they would be looking for ways to re-open the drug routes to America. This would provide great opportunities to infiltrate their operations at multiple levels. The idea was to not take down the cartel leadership until the leadership had exhausted all its avenues to ship drugs to America. It would be a seriously huge operation.

The NSA did a great job of not mentioning where or how they came by the information they passed to the joint task force. They dribbled the intel out piecemeal. But, little by little the cartel was losing, asset after asset. Every time they shifted their shipments around, they would only get a few runs and then, the DEA was there. It was a seriously bad string of luck for the cartels. The cartels paid off DEA agents had no idea where the intel was coming from, and it seemed to be random. But the cartel was consistently losing shipments on an unprecedented scale. This went on for almost two years. Then suddenly, over the course of a few months, the encrypted messages slowed to a trickle. A joint team meeting was called, and it was decided that they would leave the drug cartel's leadership intact. They had plenty of intel from the messages to tell them how to place undercover operatives in the cartel now. Changing the cartel's leadership would mean starting over from square one again in the drug war. This way, at least they still had their toe in the door.

In the fall John and Rhonda took a trip back down to Houston. They wanted to visit with some of their old friends. Sunday, they visited Splendora First Baptist Church. They had attended and served there for many years before they moved away. It was great seeing everyone. They went to lunch at a local restaurant and had a meal with some of their old church friends. Sunday evening, they drove through their old neighborhood. It hadn't changed much. They stopped at one of their long-time neighbor's house and visited with them. Monday morning John phoned Luke from the hotel phone and invited him to lunch. They agreed to meet at the China Bear restaurant on interstate 45. It was a large Chinese buffet with huge buffet tables. They met Luke in the parking lot and went inside.

John asked about McGuire and a few others he had worked with at the CIA. Luke had recently been promoted to team lead and McGuire was rumored to be planning on retiring before the end of the year. Then John asked Luke what ever happened to the bogus encryption program. Luke told him how the Russian hacker had been tricked in to stealing the program from a company that didn't really exist, how the cartel had been tipped that the Russian hacker had the program, how the hacker had asked for too much money, and the cartel had killed him and took the program. He told John how the program and back door password had been passed to the NSA, and how the drug cartels were being devastated with lost drug and money shipments over the past two years.

It sounded like the plan had worked better than expected and best of all, outside of Luke and McGuire, there was no way to trace the bogus encryption program back to him. Good news all the way around.

"John, you should have seen the fit McGuire threw about you. He really made a scene. He said you had turned your back on us for the last time. Everybody got the idea, loud and clear, never to mention the name John Davidson while around McGuire. And you thought my hillbilly cameo was priceless. I'm not sure what he was really blowing off steam about. But no one wanted to see him for a few days."

John laughed at the thought of McGuire losing it and making a scene.

"Tell McGuire, I'll see him again."

"Do I have to?"

They laughed again.

Tuesday morning John and Rhonda headed down to Alvin, Texas. John had a cousin and uncle that lived there. Alvin was south of Houston, and they had been staying in a hotel north of Houston. The drive through Houston was just as he had remembered it, high speed bumper cars. They made it through the traffic unscathed and were soon on the south side of Houston. They visited and had lunch before heading back north to their hotel room in Conroe.

John had reached out to a few of the utility guys still working in his old IT group and invited them to dinner at a Saltgrass restaurant across interstate 45 from the Woodlands. Many years before, they had all eaten there on several occasions when Don McCarthy was over the group.

Mark Harvey, Harry Dillon, and James Crain joined them for lunch. John wanted to hear how everyone was doing and they wanted to hear about him. John told them about having to move to Gulf Shores and how they were now back in Arkansas. He didn't give them the details, just the broad strokes. Since he had been a remote worker for the utility company for most of that time, He didn't have to delve into the CIA business. When asked, he told them he was working on a government job with an old high school friend, building a computer lab for research. They enjoyed the meal and said their goodbyes. Mark Harvey hung back and obviously wanted to speak with John.

When the others had left Mark said. "Hey, I always wondered what ever happened to the Luke Morgan guy?"

"You're not going to believe this, but he and I are friends. I had lunch with him Wednesday and he and I have even worked on some projects together."

"After what you did to him? But he worked for the CIA?"

"Yes, he does."

"So, you work for the CIA now?"

"No, I did some things for them. But they wanted too much from me. So, we parted ways."

"But you said you were working on a government thing."

"I am. It's just not for the CIA."

"Oh."

"I'm helping them with computer stuff. I should hear something soon about helping them with a project to build a new AI server for data searches."

"Man, that sounds like fun. Let me know if you need any help."

"Will do."

They said their goodbyes and left the restaurant. The next day John, Rhonda and Sassy headed north, back to Arkansas.

Chapter 23

~

It was mid-October, and the leaves were starting to turn. John always looked forward to this time of the year. He was sipping his morning coffee and looking out the back window towards the field when he got a text message on his phone. It was from an unknown phone number. It said. 'Check your front porch. Enjoy, Big Mac. John looked out the front window. There was no one on the porch and no cars in the driveway or street. Big Mac was the code name he and Luke used to refer to McGuire. John eased the front door open to find a long slender box leaned up against the wall near the front door. It was surprisingly heavy.

John took the box inside and inspected it. There were no labels or markings of any kind on the outside of the box. John took out his pocketknife and gently separated the glued flaps on the box. Inside was a gun case and a sheet of paper with just one word on it 'Thanks'. John opened the case to find a custom rifle. It was a Sako TRG 22 A1 chambered in 6.5 Creedmoor, with just about every accessory you can get for a gun like this. In fact, there had been some custom work done on this gun to tune it up. The tuning was done by Jack Crow, the guy who had run the CIA gun range in Houston for many years. McGuire had just asked Jack to buy a gun for John and make sure it was something that would challenge him.

There was a scrap of paper inside the gun case. It was actually part of a paper target. Jack Crow had placed it there. There were three holes cut in the paper. All of them touching. They all could easily be covered with a quarter.

John was stunned. The gun itself was about $5,000, not to mention the Steiner gun scope (easily $2,000), the gun case, extra magazines, by-pod, and other goodies. John had heard about these high precision guns, but he never had shot one, much less dreamed of owning one. The scrap of target paper had to be from Jack Crow. He was the only gun nut John had met at the CIA offices in Houston. John had the ballistics for the 243-bullet trajectory memorized. The 6.5 Creedmoor would have a totally different trajectory and maximum effective range. John would have to study the ballistics and practice at different ranges to get comfortable with the gun.

Several weeks earlier, McGuire had finally decided to retire from his career at the CIA. But, before he left, he felt there was a debt to be paid. John Davidson had placed himself and his family in danger on more than one occasion for the CIA. It was time to reward his dedication to doing what was right. McGuire took the afternoon to go to the gun range. Ever since he had moved out of active field ops and started the desk job, he had rarely made time to visit the gun range. He and Jack Crow were old friends.

"Well, well. Lookey here who decided to crawl out from under the desk. McGuire, do you even remember how to shoot that thing on your hip?"

"Great to see you, Jack. It's been way too long. Sorry about that. They just don't let me off the chain much anymore."

"I tell ya', it's tough all over, brother. What brings you to my range?"

"I need a gun."

"Are you actually planning on finally learning how to shoot?"

"Funny. No, it's a gun for someone you've had on the range before. John Davidson."

"What does he need a gun for? Did he lose his little 243 tack driver?"

"No, this is part of the price for us using him all these years. I want to get him a gun that will challenge him to keep doing better. I have no idea what kind of rifle he'd want. I suppose something for long range shooting. He seemed to like that sort of thing."

"I see. How much you want to spend on this long-range rig?"

"Don't try to break the bank, but just get him something really nice to shoot. We owe him. Send the bill to me. I'll make sure you get reimbursed. When you have the gun ready to ship give me a call. I'll have it delivered to his house."

"Cool. Hey, you think you could maybe buy one for me too?"

"Jack how many guns do you own?"

"Always one less than I need."

"Thanks Jack. Make sure it's tuned and ready to use when he gets it. Set it up like you'd want for yourself, OK?'

"Sure, sure. Did you come here to shoot or talk?"

"I really need to get back to the office."

"I'll let you know when I have the new rig put together and ready to ship."

They said goodbye and McGuire went back to his office. On the way he thought he probably should have taken the opportunity to fire a few rounds.

Two weeks had passed since their trip to Texas. Kevin and Pamela Baxley had become regulars on Sunday in the Truth Seekers Life Group class. After class John asked Kevin if he might like to go to the gun range and do a little shooting. John hadn't got to practice in almost a year now and he had a new gun to play with. He also needed to make sure he still knew where his shooting skill limits were.

The following Monday, Kevin met John at the gun range at 4:00. There was only one other person on the range. They went to the pistol range and shot for a while, then they moved to the long-distance range. They had this range to themselves. John drove to the 100 and 200 yard heavy metal targets and spray painted them white. Then he placed a hi-vis orange dot sticker in the center of each. Normally he would have used a target with a one-inch grid line background. That gave him specific data on how far he was off target. But today was mostly just a fun day to plink some targets. Not really to tune skills.

John retrieved a gun case with the 243 in it and an ammo box from the rear of his Rubicon. He let Kevin carry the sandbags and ear protectors. The night before John had studied the ballistics charts for the Creedmoor round. He was a little disappointed in what he found. The ballistics for the Creedmoor bullet was not much different than his old 243. But, he had to admit this was a much cooler looking gun.

John took the first three shots out of his trusty 243 at the 200-yard target. The hits were well within his personal limits. All shots were less than two inches away from the orange dot. Not his best. But it had been a year since he had done any target shooting.

Kevin shot the gun at the 200-yard target and did very well for never having fired the gun before. With a little practice he might be better than John. They had worked their way through a box of ammo and John was itching to try out his new gun.

"Hey man, I have a brand-new gun I want to try out, let's get it out and see what we can do with it."

John packed the 243 back into its gun case and took it back to the Rubicon. When he came back, he had the gun case with the new rifle in it. He removed the Sako TRG 22 A1 from the case and attached the by-pod to the front. As he placed the gun on the shooting bench, he was again impressed with just how totally sexy this beast of a gun looked. It just looked bad to the bone.

"Wow! That's a serious looking gun. I bet that set you back a few bucks."

"Not really, it was a gift. But I did have to pay a pretty steep price for it. I'll tell you about it some time."

They shot and despite John's unfamiliarity with the gun, it was clear the groups were much tighter than those with his old 243 hunting rifle. With some practice, John could extend his personal shooting distance limits with this gun. Unless you are shooting a cannon, it was mostly about good bullet placement at long distances. With this gun that would be a little easier to manage.

They shot a box of the 5.6 Creedmoor rounds and then called it a day and headed home. One thing was clear. John would need to put in some serious time on the gun range before he was able to fully use the capabilities of this gun. The extra precision came at a price. For the money, John would have stayed with the 243. But this was a gift, so game on.

While cleaning the guns that evening, John thought when he got proficient enough, he would have to send Jack Crow a target of his own. John whispered to himself 'Challenge accepted Jack Crow'.

Chapter 24

~

Tuesday morning John had a sticky note on his computer keyboard that indicated Director Jill Stephens wanted to see him. Before he logged on to the workstation, he got a cup of coffee and went to her office.

"John, they gave us the money for the AI server."

"That sounds like good news for the lab."

"Now, it's your turn to do your part. We're going to be putting up some walls in the computer lab. When it's finished, we will have a ten by twelve-foot size room just for the AI server. We're going to harden the room to keep everything that happens in that room secure, and it will be built electronically sealed".

John knew that electronically sealed meant the room would be shielded from all radio, cellular, and microwave transmissions. This was going to be an expensive build.

"Ms. Stephens, we might do better to spend some of that money on the computer hardware, like faster processors, more memory, larger disk arrays. That sort of stuff will improve the AI functions which will translate to faster and deeper data searches."

"John, let me worry about the money and you worry about building the AI. Get a hardware list together for me. The construction will be finished in three weeks, and I want all the hardware delivered and ready to set up by then. Are you going to need any additional resources for the build."

John thought for a moment. "I need four hours in Houston and four hours at Langley Airforce Base to inventory some up and running AI computer labs."

"Can you get that done this week?"

"Yes."

"See Jackie on you way out for the travel arrangements, I'll expect to have the hardware list and start ordering equipment Monday."

"Yes sir, mam." John said with a grin and a salute.

She couldn't help but grin. "Get going! I have work to do."

John phoned Ms. Ricky Roberts and asked if he could tour the CIA's AI computer lab again. She made the arrangements to get him in there for about 30 minutes during lunch.

Next, he phoned Robert Saunders at Langley Airforce Base. Robert was going to be out of the office, but he arranged to get one of his guys to meet John at the security gate and escort him on a quick tour of the NSA AI computer lab.

Next John went to Jackie's desk and told her the dates and times he needed to be at each of the sites. She booked his flights, rental cars, and a hotel near Norfolk International airport.

That evening for dinner John and Rhonda had an old family favorite, 'Cheese and Frank Creole'. They diced onion, bell pepper, and hotdogs. These were added to a skillet with butter. After a few minutes they added the diced mushroom, petite diced tomatoes, and spices. This was allowed to simmer for ten minutes while they made some toast with cheese melted on it. The skillet mixture was poured over the cheese toast and served. It was a simple but delicious dinner. As they were eating John told Rhonda about his travel plans.

The next morning John got dressed, grabbed his old leather portfolio, and headed to the Little Rock airport. His first trip was a direct flight to and from Houston. It was going to be a long day. But at least he'd be home, sleeping in his own bed tonight.

He drove from the George Bush Intercontinental Airport to the CIA's Houston offices. He met Ms. Ricky Roberts in the lobby. She gave him a visitor's badge. Per security procedures a visitor was required to be with an escort at all times. From the lobby they went straight to the AI lab where John was handed off to a tech guy in the lab. This time John was paying attention to and asking questions about the hardware. John made notes on the scratchpad in his portfolio. As he was looking the hardware over he saw something that caught his eye. It was a small extra piece between the keyboard's USB plug and the computer. It really just looked like a slightly long USB plug end. It was not obvious. But John had seen a device like this on a YouTube video on spy gadgets. If this was the same type of device, then it was a key logger. Someone was recording every keystroke on this keyboard. John was no expert, but he knew not to blurt out what he suspected.

John had all of the info on the AI computer lab's equipment he needed. John checked his cell phone, no bars. That meant this room was shielded, no signals in or out.

"I guess we're done here. Can I stop by and see director Roberts again? I would like to thank her before I leave."

"Sure, her office is just down the hall."

"Man, that was a long flight, is there a restroom I can use first?"

John knew from his previous visit that there was a bathroom just around the corner.

"No problem. It's right over here. I'll wait out here for you."

Once in the bathroom John went into a stall and closed the door. He tore a page out of the tablet in his portfolio, scribbled a quick note to Ms. Roberts, and folded it in half.

He exited the bathroom, and his escort took him to director Robert's office. She was alone and reading something on her computer screen. She stood as John entered the room.

John extended his hand, and she shook it.

"I just wanted to stop by and say thank you.

"John, did you get everything you needed?"

"Yes mam, and then some. Well, I have to catch a plane pretty soon so, until we meet again."

In one fluid motion, as John released the handshake, he snagged the note from his portfolio, laid it on the edge of her desk, turned and left the room. Per security protocol the escort had to follow John to the lobby.

Director Roberts retrieved the handwritten note from the far side of her desk, unfolded and read it.

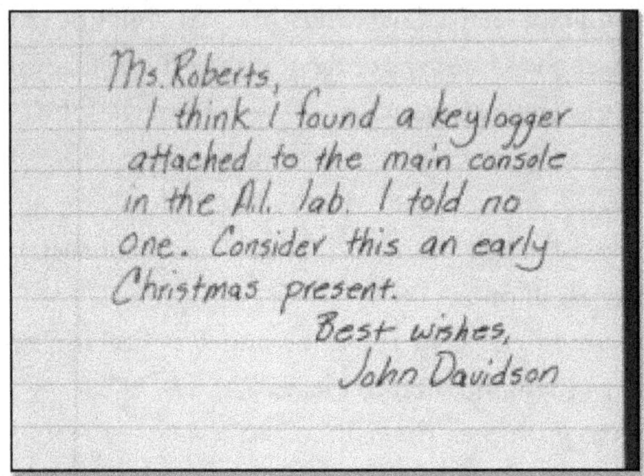

Suddenly she had a sick feeling in her gut. There was a rat in the computer lab, and she hated rats. First to verify the keylogger was in fact in there. Then it would be time to build a rat trap.

She phoned Luke Morgan in operations and asked him to come see her when he had the time. Luke was in field operations. But he had started out as a electronics tech with modest computer skills. She needed someone from the outside to verify the problem, if there was one. She would let everyone believe she was trying to steal Luke away from the field ops group.

In a few minutes he was knocking on her door. She had requested his personnel file and had it open on her desk. To anyone passing by it looked all together like an interview. She said, "Come in and have a seat."

"Luke are you still up on the latest gadgets.?"

"Yes, it's a hobby of mine. Why?"

"I need a favor. What do you know about key loggers?"

She showed him the note John had passed her.

"Wow, that sucks."

"I need you to find it and bait a trap for me. I have to catch this rat red handed."

"Hmmm, I have a pin hole camera that would work great."

"The room is shielded."

"OK, I don't think that's going to matter with this camera. A friend of mine at DARPA (Defense Advanced Research Projects Agency) loaned it to me for testing. It stores the photos and when you get in range with a cellphone, it auto downloads all the pictures to your cell phone. It's ultra small and perfect for this type of scenario. Let me run back to my desk and get it. I'll need a few minutes in the server room to verify the key logger and set everything up."

"Sounds like a good plan, Luke. But let's keep this between just you and me for now. If anyone asks, tell them I am trying to get you to take a job in our computer lab. I actually do have a position open, if you're interested?"

"I'll be back in a flash" and Luke left her office. Thirty minutes later it was lunch time and most of the people had left for lunch. No one was in the AI computer lab when Roberts and Luke entered. Luke found the key logger and inspected it. It was very small. But Luke had actually seen one of these. They had a built-in memory to store the keystrokes. He left it in place after taking a few photographs of it.

"Yes mam. It's a key logger alright. What was John in here for?"

"Doesn't matter. Can you tell how long it's been in here?"

"Yes, but I'd need to remove it and download the keystroke data."

"I'll get that done later."

Next, Luke pulled a chair to the center of the room to place the small camera in the florescent light fixture. He had to drill a small hole in the frame that kept the diffuser panel in place. He pulled a small drill from his jacket pocket. He used a piece of paper to catch the shavings as he drilled. He pushed one of the suspended ceiling tiles aside and positioned the camera in the space above the ceiling, over the pinhole he had just made. He carefully folded the paper with the shaving in it and pocketed it along with the small drill motor. He replaced the ceiling tile, jumped off the chair, wiped his shoe prints from the chair's seat cushion and replaced the chair exactly as he found it. He pulled his cell phone out and after a few minutes showed Roberts a picture of him cleaning the seat cushion. The main console was center frame. Anyone using this terminal or grabbing the key logger would be photographed.

Roberts checked her watch. Six minutes since they stepped into the AI Computer lab. That was fast, considering.

"How often do you think they download the key logger data?"

Luke tried to remember the memory capacity of the similar device he had seen. "It depends on how much the main console is used. "

"I'm not sure but I think it's used at least six times every day. We get lots of request for deep data searches."

"My guess is that they probably download the key log data every few days. That key logger is super small and made to match up with the end of the USB cord. It's like it was specially made just for that keyboard. I wouldn't have noticed it, if you hadn't told me, it was there. How did John see it?"

"John doesn't see things the way we do. He's weird that way. Tell me about the camera."

"I'll text you a link to a download. Install the android app on your phone. It will want a password. Use 'ICU812' all in caps. When you want to download the pictures, start the application, enter the password 'ICU812' all in caps and walk into the computer lab. It should auto send all of the pictures it has taken to your phone. You'll need to be in the computer lab a minimum of five minutes to ensure all of the photos are transferred to your phone. When you get the photos you need, give me a call. I will have to return that camera to my buddy at DARPA."

"Thanks, Luke. Maybe I can return the favor someday."

"Just doin' my job mam, just doin' my job."

Luke left the computer lab and went back to his office. As team lead, he had reports to do.

Roberts decided she would find an excuse to be in the computer lab a few times every week. With any luck they'd have the rat in a trap by the end of the week.

John was met at the Newport News/Williamsburg International Airport baggage claim by the same straight-faced corporal as before. It was going to be another boring drive to the Langley Airforce base in silence. John was greeted by Robert Saunders, the director of the NSA computer lab.

"John, great to see you again. What can we do for you?"

"I thought you were going to be out of town?"

"The meeting got postponed."

"I need some specs on the hardware you guys used for the AI lab server. I'm going to help the FBI build their own AI based server room."

"Wow! Well, we can help with that. I will need some guarantee that you're not going to use this information against us."

"You can call my boss if you like. I would, in your position." John handed Robert a business card for Director Jill Stephens of the FBI. Robert handed the card back to John. "She called yesterday and said you were coming for a tour of our computer lab."

They headed to the computer lab. John got the hardware specifications of their AI server and disk arrays. He also made a note of the base software they were using for security and communications in the lab. When he had all the information he needed, John followed Robert to a conference room adjacent to Robert's office. As John entered the room the aroma of savory food reminded him that he hadn't gotten to eat anything since dinner the night before. The conference room table was covered with a white tablecloth. On it were various trays of sandwiches, wraps and even some hot food trays that were kept warm with a small can of gel fuel burning below them. There was ice, coffee, tea, water, and cans of soda. On a separate table there were a dozen slices of various cakes and pies to choose from.

"Wow! All for me?" John, figured he'd find out soon what this lavish lunch was all about.

"You're going to complain because we fed you?"

"Nope." With that John grabbed a plate and started filling it.

They were alone, eating lunch in a conference room. "John, why build an AI lab when you've got one right here. If you want, you can just come to work for us. We have some cutting-edge AI software in that lab. It was developed especially for us at some think tank. It's several generations ahead of anything you'll have at the FBI."

"That sounds very enticing, and I sure would love working with your guys, and playing with your AI systems here; the wife and I are just tired of moving around. In Arkansas we have family and friends; it's where we grew up. In Texas, and even more so in Alabama, seeing family and old friends was a very rare occasion. We're just tired of moving and want to stay put for a while."

Robert had run a background check on John using the NSA's AI server. The NSA had access to all CIA and FBI files. Robert had above average reading and comprehension skills. He didn't have a photographic memory. But he quickly digested the thick report on John's history beginning with where he grew up, his parents, schooling, his work at the utility company, the Prophet X program, the CIA, and now the FBI. John had an adventurous life.

"John, the door is always open, should you change your mind. Now, let's check out the desserts. I want to try one of those pies. They tell me they are to die for."

After a slice of delicious triple berry pie, they shook hands and John found his escort standing outside the door. As it turned out, he would spend the night in a hotel near the airport and catch the first flight out in the morning.

By the time the plane landed in Little Rock the next day, John had compiled a hardware list for the FBI's new AI lab. He had used most of the hardware the NSA had, but with some minor alterations. He had looked up similar components on the web and estimated the hardware cost. He had no idea how much money was available for the project. So, he researched and found some cheaper component options that he hoped would have little impact on the speed or capabilities of the new AI system. He would review his recommendation and forward it to FBI director Jill Stephens the day after he got home.

The various pieces of computer equipment arrived over the next three weeks and before long John had everything connected and tested. Over the next few months John spent many hours in the FBI's new AI server room, modifying code, adding, and modifying routines, building data connections to various government databases and report archives. He had gotten access to state police, city, county, and court room data bases. He had limited access to the CIA databases. He really wanted access to the NSA and Echelon databases. But there were people blocking it. Next, he went to the private sector; he requested and got access to various domain servers, Verizon, AT&T, Google, Apple, and Facebook data. There were no phones in the room, and it had been constructed with a special signal blocking copper mesh in the floor, ceiling and walls. The consoles and servers had intrusion detection built into their systems. When a thumb drive or any device was plugged into the system it would automatically lock the doors and shut down the server. The door could only then be opened from outside via special security clearance. The only connection to the outside world that the AI server had was through a special packet inspection interface. It inspected and routed all requests to receive or send data to or from the server room. It was a highly specialized intrusion detection and communications server. It had parameters that allowed only specific types of data to or from the AI server.

Chapter 25

~

One Saturday morning John found himself sitting on the back porch, watching the woods in the field. The mornings were getting cooler, the summer heat was subsiding, and fall would soon arrive. He was thinking about all that had happened, and all of the ways God had protected and blessed him and Rhonda. It was odd that just as they seemed to get settled in somewhere, God would move them elsewhere. Perhaps they were not meant to settle, but to move where God would lead them. But, then again, perhaps God had been moving them back home all along. John's mother was doing well despite having to take chemo for her cancer every few weeks. She had made new friends at church after John's dad had passed away. She was always busy doing something with her friends from church. John wondered how long the Lord might let them stay settled this time.

John decided it was time to work with the new rifle. He sure wasn't going to improve his shooting with it by sitting on the back porch. After breakfast John loaded up the Jeep for the gun range. Over the course of the next few months, John managed to get about twenty practice sessions on the gun range. The Sako TRG 22 A1 chambered in 6.5 Creedmoor was much more accurate than John's shooting ability. He finally found a custom load and a factory load that the gun seemed to shoot consistently. Next, he started working his way out on the long range. In the end he decided he would stick with the two-hundred-yard range. He would only shoot at further targets to verify the trajectory at different ranges.

After three months of shooting the gun, John phoned McGuire.

"Hello?"

"McGuire, this is John Davidson."

"Man, I was just fixing to leave the dock to do a little fishing. How are you and the family doing? I hope you're not in trouble again. Because I'm retired."

"No, we're doing fine. Everything is pretty routine up here. I wanted to thank you for the rifle and see if you have an mailing address for Jack Crow? I want to send him something."

"It was the least I could do for you. And yes, I have his address. Can I text it to you at this number?"

"Yes, perfect. Thanks, and good luck with the fishing. I'll let you get to it then. Thanks again!"

"Goodbye."

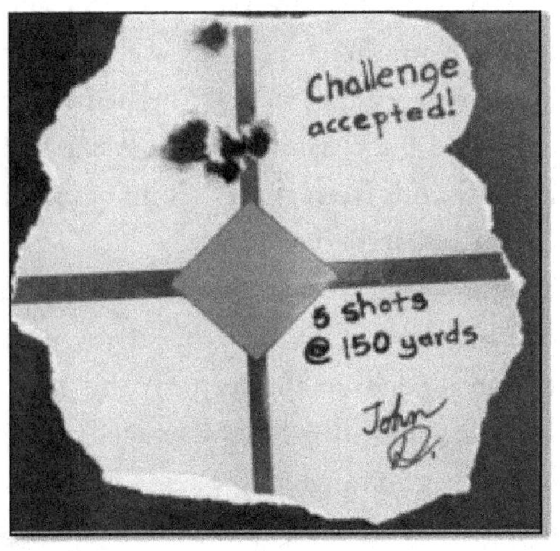

A few minutes later John had Jack Crows mailing address on his phone. It was time to send Jack Crow a message. He had shot better groupings with the rifle. But after shooting, he typically just noted the size of the groupings along with ammunition type, temperature, humidity, and wind readings in his shooting diary. The paper targets went to the trash when he got home. But he saved this one for Jack Crow. He had the gun tuned for 200 yards. He always used it as a zero for his long guns. He had hoped the group would be much tighter at

150 yards. But it was good enough to answer Crow's challenge. He dropped a large envelope into the mail with Jack Crow's address on it. In the envelope were just two scraps of paper. He mailed his 150-yard target and the 100-yard target Jack Crow had sent with the gun. In John's estimation he was about 90% on the new gun. He might slowly improve with more practice. But he was confident in his limitations with the new gun and pretty much knew the bullet drop was within any reasonable range. He always equated his personal limits to deer hunting as it had been such a constant since he could hold a gun.

Over the course of the next six months, John settled down to a simi regular routine. He worked a regular forty-hour week, he was home every night, Rhonda was still working from home in corporate travel. Saturdays they worked in the yard and sometimes went out to eat with friends. On Sundays they were almost always in church. Their lives were almost normal.

John's work at the FBI's new Artificial Intelligence Lab was becoming routine as well. He ran the deep data searches, tweaking the search engines as he went. In just a few minutes he could retrieve reams of information on almost anyone. If they lived in the state, then he knew almost everything there was to know about them. But the most beneficial data came from the AI system's ability to connect people. Having an accurate, up to date list of known associates was key to many of their investigations.

Their kids were doing well in college. Daniel was still settling into college life at Texas A&M and undecided on his major. Amanda was having fun in her new life at Arkansas State University at Jonesboro. Her current major was Disaster Preparedness/Emergency Management. She wanted to be an Emergency Medical Technician.

~ The End ~

About the Author

~

David Johnson was born and raised in small town in central Arkansas. His early life experiences revolved around church, family, hunting, fishing, and water sports. As a young man he married and began a career with the local utility company. As computers became prevalent in the workplace, David discovered a gift for understanding computers and in particular writing computer programs. His career spans over twenty-five years employed in the computer field, writing computer programs, database design, developing Internet based applications, and various web sites. He was blessed to be able to work with the latest in computer, server, and Internet technologies.

David Johnson is a Christian and enjoys studying the Bible and reading various texts on the Bible. He is an ordained Deacon who remains actively involved in many of the activities at his local church. He enjoys artwork, writing, and working in the yard.

David's wife has worked in banking and corporate travel for many years. Her career has afforded them travel experiences in many other countries, some of which included Mexico, the Caribbean and various places throughout Europe.

David and his wife enjoy swimming, motorcycle rides, camping, kayaking, and SCUBA diving when they are not attending church or visiting with family.

About the Book Series

~

Thank you for purchasing *'New Beginnings'*. I hope you enjoyed reading it as much as I enjoyed writing it.

I would be remiss if I didn't take this opportunity to thank my family and friends for putting up with me while I write. I do tend to enjoy telling others about the story as it develops.

'Legacy' is the third book in this series and is available for purchase. To learn more about the development of this book please go to the following link:

http://www.davidandrhonda.com/book-web/index.htm

Did you love *New Beginnings - Book 2*? Then you should read *Legacy - Book 3*[1] by David Johnson!

The third book ("Legacy") is about John Davidson's son (Daniel). Daniel is approached for an experimental program in the CIA. The program identifies and enhances certain skill sets that are useful in certain types of field operations. The training is unique, demanding physically and mentally. This is much different than his college life was. As he works with SEALs teams, his reputation grows. A foreign crime syndicate makes the deadly mistake of trying to coerce him into stealing military weapons. Through a near death experience Daniel realizes he can no longer go it alone. He needs divine help to survive.

Read more at www.DavidAndRhonda.com/book-new/index.htm.

---

1. https://books2read.com/u/4NDkoN

2. https://books2read.com/u/4NDkoN

About the Author

David Johnson was born and raised in a small town in central Arkansas. Early life experiences revolved around church, family, hunting, fishing, and water sports. As a young man he married and began a career with the local utility company. For over 22 years he was employed as a Software Engineer, writing computer programs, and developing Internet-based applications and web sites. He has worked with the latest in programming and Internet technologies

Read more at www.davidandrhonda.com/book-web/index.htm.